W9-CBS-854

MIKE HAMEL's MATTERHORN the BRAVE

No. 2

Talis Hunters

Christian Shoemaker
8500 Prestina Pl NE
Albuquerque, NM   87111

MIKE HAMEL's
MATTERHORN the BRAVE
No. 2

Talis Hunters

LIVING INK BOOKS
Writing Worth Reading

Talis Hunters
Matterhorn the Brave™ Series: Volume 2
Copyright © 2007 by Mike Hamel
Published by AMG Publishers
6815 Shallowford Rd.
Chattanooga, Tennessee 37421

All rights reserved. Except for brief quotations in printed reviews, no part of this publication may be reproduced, stored in a retrieval system, or transmitted in any form or by any means (printed, written, photocopied, visual electronic, audio, or otherwise) without the prior permission of the publisher.

Published in association with the literary agency of Sanford Communications, Inc., 16778 S.E. Cohiba Ct., Damascus, OR 97089

MATTERHORN THE BRAVE is a trademark of CLW Communications Group, Inc.

ISBN: 978-089957834-7
First printing—January 2007
Cover illustration: Mike Salter (Chattanooga, TN)
Cover design: Daryle Beam (Chattanooga, TN)
Interior design and typesetting by Reider Publishing Services,
    West Hollywood, California
Edited and proofread by Pat Matuszak, Sharon Neal, Dan Penwell, and
    Rick Steele

Printed in Canada
13 12 11 10 09 08 07 –T– 8 7 6 5 4 3 2 1

Library of Congress Cataloging-in-Publication Data
Hamel, Mike.
    The talis hunters / Mike Hamel. -- Rev. ed.
        p. cm. -- (Matterhorn the brave series ; v. 2)
    Summary: In his second adventure, Matterhorn finds himself transported by the Maker 13,000 years into the past, and, along with Aaron the Baron, Princess Jewels, and Nate the Great, must find the talis that the Sasquatch are guarding.
    ISBN-13: 978-0-89957-834-7 (pbk. : alk. paper)
    [1. Sasquatch--Fiction. 2. Space and time--Fiction. 3. Christian life--Fiction. 4. Science fiction.] I. Title.
    PZ7.H176Tal 2007
    [Fic]--dc22
                                                    2006039528

The characters and stories in this
series exist because of Susan,
who made them all possible.

Contents

Prologue 1

Chapter 1   Royal Reunion 7

Chapter 2   Indian Heaven 11

Chapter 3   Troubled Realm 16

Chapter 4   Unexpected Guest 21

Chapter 5   Morning Briefing 26

Chapter 6   Three Faces West 31

Chapter 7   U-turn 36

Chapter 8   Moose Meadow 41

Chapter 9   Raging River 45

Chapter 10   Special Delivery 50

Chapter 11   Leap of Faith 55

Chapter 12   Water Landing 61

Chapter 13   Open Sesame 65

Chapter 14   Spelunker's Paradise 70

Chapter 15   Tunnel of Doom 75

Chapter 16   Break Point 79

Chapter 17   Dark Spirits 83

Chapter 18   Green Giants 88

Chapter 19   Seymour and the Band 93

Chapter 20   Wave Pool 98

Chapter 21   ER 103

Chapter 22   Enemy Territory 108

Chapter 23   Good Medicine 114

Chapter 24   Color Line 119

Chapter 25   Blown Assignment 126

Chapter 26   Ambush 131

Chapter 27   Vital Link 135

Chapter 28   Friendly Persuasion 140

Chapter 29   Peace Offering 145

Chapter 30   Upward Exodus 150

Chapter 31   Ensnared 155

Chapter 32   Unnecessary Roughness 160

Chapter 33   Self-Defense 165

Chapter 34   Forced March 170

Chapter 35   Emergency Exit 174

Epilogue 178

Prologue

THE Monday after Matthew Horn returned from Ireland, he arrived at school by 6:30 a.m. When the custodian unlocked the doors, Matt mumbled something about an unfinished assignment and begged to be let into the library. Once there, he headed straight for Mr. Rickets. With shaking hands, Matt pulled out *The Sword and the Flute*. He sat on the floor and speed-read it once more.

How these words got into the once-blank book wasn't the only question on Matt's mind. He wanted to know if there were other stories among Mr. Ricket's treasures that had "holes" in them. Carefully at first, then more frantically, he checked every book. All of them seemed normal.

When Miss Tull showed up an hour later, Matt strolled over to her desk and asked his favorite librarian, "Is there anything special about the books on Mr. Rickets?"

"All books are special," she replied with a smile that tilted the glasses on her long nose.

"Have you read these?" Matt asked, trying to sound casual.

"Most."

"How about *The Sword and the Flute*?"

Gray eyes locked onto him over the top of her specs. "You must be mistaken," she replied. "There is no such title."

Matt showed her the book.

She frowned and said, "Hmm, I will have to enter it into the catalog. What is it about?"

Matt stepped back from this question, mumbling something about getting to class. No sense having Miss Tull concerned over his sanity. He hadn't even told his parents about what had happened.

The next few days he poked around Mr. Rickets whenever Miss Tull wasn't looking. He was dying to find a way back to the Propylon. He needed to know if Queen Bea had made it home with Ian's Flute. Were there other Talis on Earth that needed finding? Would the Sword summon him to help find them?

Evidently not.

Life went on as it had before his adventure. Eventually, Matt gave up searching for portals. However, he did decide to prepare himself in case he was called upon again. Since he was now a knight, he would learn how to handle a sword. He read books on fencing and checked into martial arts built around swordplay such as *aikido* and *kenjutsu*. He even discovered the Society for Creative Anachronism, a group that recreated medieval jousts and tournaments. Finally he settled on *Kendo*, the Way of the Sword.

No one in his family understood Matt's sudden interest in swords. His mom worried about injuries. His dad expected him to tire of the training and discipline involved. But they both knew that once Matt got an idea into his head, he was more stubborn than crabgrass. And so they signed the permission slip and bought the uniform, the body armor, and several *shinai*—bamboo practice swords.

For the next few months, Matt went to the *dojo* every day after school. He skipped indoor soccer and focused on kendo. He worked hard on his eye-hand coordination, practicing attacks and defenses as though his life depended on it.

One day it might.

The seasons worked their way around to spring. On a fresh Friday afternoon, Matt came home from school, changed clothes, grabbed his pack, and headed for The Loft. The Loft was an eight-foot-square tree house nestled in the heart of an ancient apple tree. Matt had helped Vic and his dad build it many years ago. It perched six feet off the ground, which was plenty high for Matt. Thick branches and lush leaves shielded it from prying eyes while still letting in lots of sun.

This marvel of backyard engineering had been built without pounding a single nail into the venerable tree. It had running water—a plastic jug that tipped into a bucket sink at the pull of a rope—and even a garden-level basement made by hanging tarps from floor to ground.

Matt scrambled up the ladder and plopped into a scrunchy green beanbag. He had checked out *The Sword and the Flute* to reread of his adventures with Aaron the Baron. Halfway through the book, he heard a faint hissing, like air being sucked through a tiny straw. The noise was coming from a period on the page in front of him.

The spot of ink was growing.

Matt's eyes grew bigger along with it.

A portal?

At long last!

For months Matt had dreamed of this moment. Now he panicked. Butterflies banged into each other in his stomach. Beads of sweat called an emergency meeting on his forehead. His feet wanted to head straight for his bedroom.

He had almost not returned from his first tumble into a portal. Pirates had tried to kill him and a dark spirit had almost succeeded. If he knew what was good for him, he would run to the house; he would stay put in the present where it was safe.

Why would he risk taking another plunge into the unknown?

The answer came to him with caffeine clarity.

Because the Sword of Truth was calling.

Because he was the Queen's Knight.

Because he had sworn to serve the Maker.

Because he would not ignore his destiny.

The spot on the page had grown to the size of a CD. Matt could detect the swirling; he could feel the pull. His muscles tensed in anticipation. He patted his pockets to make sure he had his quote book and harmonica. Satisfied, he pressed his palms together, tucked his head and leaned forward.

First came the tingling in his fingertips then the painless stretching.

Matt had been unwittingly sucked through his first portal and deposited in a heap of arms and legs. This time he would make a better entrance. He would somersault his body as he passed through the portal and come out the other end like a superhero.

Fat chance.

Royal Reunion

MATTERHORN the Brave came rolling from the cave like candy out of a gumball machine. When the skittering mass of elbows and kneecaps came to rest, a red head popped up from the tangle of limbs. Hazel green eyes blinked open and took in the surroundings. Stately Sitka spruce and bushy western hemlock crowded the landscape. Through their spiked green heads, Matterhorn saw the horizon being tickled pink by the setting sun.

Where was he?

When was he?

Why was he here?

An evening breeze rustled the trees and raised goose bumps on his skin. He stood and rubbed his arms for warmth. They were well muscled since the trip through the portal had accelerated him to adulthood. He had fallen in one end as a preteen and out the other as a young man with an athlete's body.

Matterhorn grinned. This physical change was one of the best things he remembered about time-space travel.

He checked his hair. Sure enough, the fire-red ponytail was back. His legs were twice their normal size, though his feet looked about the same. Not surprising since he had big feet for his age.

A good thing his clothes also grew, he thought as he dusted sticky pine needles from his pants, or he would be very uncomfortable right about now. He stretched his new muscles and did a 360. He was in the middle of nowhere and unprepared for the fast-approaching night. He didn't even have a coat, much less a tent or any way to make a fire. Aaron the Baron had been with him on his first adventure, and the Baron came equipped for every situation. From inflatable backpacks to collapsible weapons, he had more gadgets than a secret agent. Without his resourceful partner, Matterhorn felt lost.

But not for long.

First he heard the voices of two women, and then their forms emerged from the forest with arms full of firewood. He recognized the taller woman as Queen Bea of First Realm. Even without her throne and crown there was no mistaking her royal bearing. Her arrival made Matterhorn feel 1,000 percent better.

When the Queen caught sight of Matterhorn, her face crinkled into a smile. "Ah, here is my knight now. How good of you to come." She turned to her companion and said, "Princess Jewel, this is Matterhorn the Brave. Matterhorn, this is Princess Jewel."

"Yell-O," Matterhorn said.

"Hi," Jewel replied in a rich alto voice.

He had seen her once before on a computer in the Baron's workshop. She was prettier in person, with wide-awake brown eyes and cinnamon skin smoother than jeweler's felt. An onyx wolf earring dangled from her right ear. A dark flow of coffee hair ran down her back in a heavy braid. She wore buckskin pants and a leather vest over a hunter green shirt. Standing five foot five in her moccasins, she looked almost petite. Matterhorn recalled Aaron's respect for her and assumed she must be tougher than she appeared.

Jewel was sizing him up at the same time. Six foot four, she guessed, and about 210 pounds. Rangy limbs, indoor complexion, nice ponytail.

The Queen cleared her throat to regain Matterhorn's attention. "We have much to discuss and you are not the only night to arrive. Make yourself useful by finding some water. Jewel has a water skin you can fill."

Matterhorn followed the women to the beginnings of a campsite and got the skin. "There's a stream about a quarter mile beyond that bank of deer ferns," Jewel said, pointing with her chin. "Don't get lost."

She meant it. Moving downhill from the cave, Matterhorn was swallowed in a confusing riot of green. Tall trees overshadowed him as he pushed through the dozen different kinds of ferns that wrestled for space on the forest floor. Sleek squirrels eyed him warily while the more suspicious gray jays squawked in alarm. The air pulsed with evening sounds and evergreen smells.

Drawn by the gurgling, Matterhorn located the stream. His arrival startled a gang of black-tailed deer, but not the fat rainbow trout lounging in the pool. The crystal water stung his hands as he filled the skin. He remembered how the Baron taught him to squat, not kneel, at a riverbank to make him less vulnerable to attack.

Was there danger of attack here? From wild animals? Natives? Matterhorn glanced around uneasily. He liked being outdoors, but the wildness of this place unnerved him. Whistling for his courage, he started back to camp. The cheerful noise died on his lips a few moments later.

It wasn't the size of the animal that froze his face and feet, but the white racing stripes running down the creature's fur.

Staring up at him was the biggest polecat Matterhorn had ever seen. His nose wrinkled as he recalled the rank smell of the neighbor's dog after her encounter with a skunk. He had no wish to be sprayed by this mobile stink-dispenser.

As the skunk sauntered past him, Matterhorn counted four small skunks waddling in her wake. He drew on his kendo training to focus himself into perfect stillness. Momma passed close enough to brush his leg with her tail. Skunklet number three stopped and shoved its nose up Matterhorn's pant leg.

Were baby skunks armed and dangerous? He did *not* want to find out.

When the family moved on, so did Matterhorn. He retraced his footprints to camp and found Jewel busy peeling some strange-looking roots.

"You're sweating," she said, taking the water skin. "Did you have any trouble?"

"Just met a few of the neighbors."

Indian Heaven

J EWEL filled a cooking pot and placed it on the fire. She added the camas roots, along with some greens and spices. When the mix began to simmer she sprinkled in a yellow powder to thicken it.

Cornstarch, Matterhorn figured. The aroma reminded him of his mom's vegetable stew. He got comfortable and waited for supper.

"Have you been well since our last meeting?" Queen Bea asked from the other side of the fire. The light danced in her brown eyes and gave her cheeks a healthy glow. She had on loose jeans and a long-sleeve russet blouse, accented by a teardrop sapphire at her throat and a golden charm bracelet on her wrist. Her thick hair was wound into a bun at the nape of her neck. There was a small object in her right ear Matterhorn couldn't make out. A knapsack rested against her leg.

"Yes, thank you," Matterhorn said. "I was beginning to think I'd never see you again. How long has it been, anyway?"

Bea smiled. "For you, months; for me, days."

The time difference didn't come as a complete shock to Matterhorn. Uncle Al had often told him time was relative. It depended on factors like the speed and direction you happened to be going. Evidently Earth and First Realm, while being mirror worlds, were not in sync.

"What have you been doing with yourself?" the Queen asked.

"Studying kendo," Matterhorn said, pressing his palms together and bowing. "It is the Way of the Sword."

"Then I suppose you will be wanting this. It is the reason you are here." She reached down and pulled a red leather hilt from her pack. The three watched a diamond blade grow from the handle. A liquid sunbeam appeared in its center. This was the Sword of Truth, one of the Ten Talis, fashioned by the Maker to represent His integrity and truthfulness.

Matterhorn reached over and took the weapon. He noted the inscription on the silver crosspiece, etched there by the Maker: *Truth is a Blade sharp as Light.* The scritch pad was still attached to the hilt. It matched the square pad on his own belt. Scritch was the Baron's Velcro-like invention, only stronger.

Matterhorn willed the blade to vanish and stuck the hilt to the pad. In a strange way he felt whole again, as though an amputated limb had been miraculously restored.

"Did the Baron explain to you about portals and what they are used for?" Bea asked.

"Yes," Matterhorn said. "He told me your people opened portals on planets they wanted to observe. On

Earth they're in mystical places like Stonehenge and the pyramids."

"The cave you came through is also a portal. I used it to bring Jewel here this afternoon. You, of course, were summoned by the Sword."

"Summoned where?"

"Tomorrow morning, if you look above those trees, you will see how Mount St. Helens appeared before she blew her top. Over there," Bea pointed in the opposite direction, "you will see Mount Adams. Between these two giants is the very unstable piece of real estate we are sitting on. In your day it is called the Indian Heaven Volcanic Field."

That had an ominous sound to it.

"Princess Jewel is a Chinook Indian," Bea continued. "Centuries from now her people will live on this land. Her knowledge of the area will be helpful to you and the Baron."

"So will my cooking," Jewel said, handing them each a bowl of steaming stew.

"Anything is better than the Baron's cooking," Matterhorn mumbled as he took the bowl.

Jewel shot the Queen a knowing glance. "The Baron has many skills," she said. "Cooking is not among them. Where is he anyway?"

"I do not know," Bea said. "He should have arrived by now."

Conversation stopped while they ate. Matterhorn used the silence to do a quick mental review of what he had learned when his family had camped in the Pacific

Northwest last summer. The guide who took them fishing on the Columbia River had told tall tales of the Chinook, Kwakiutl, Nootka, and Tillamook tribes. The Native Americans had lived undisturbed on the banks of the big river until the white man "civilized" them onto reservations.

The Queen finished her stew and resumed her explanation. "The volcanoes in this place make it prone to earthquakes. A major one is due in the next few days, hence the urgency of your task. The quake may collapse the entrance to an underground city. One of the Ten Talis is there. You must retrieve the Talis before it is too late."

"A few days!" Matterhorn sputtered. "Couldn't we have come any earlier?"

"We do well to be here at all," Bea said. "And do not forget whom you are addressing."

"I'm sor—"

The Queen cut him off with a gesture. "I owe you an explanation since you will be risking your life."

These words fell like cold rain on Matterhorn's excitement, reminding him that he had been brought here as a soldier, not a tourist.

Bea became strangely silent. A single tear formed on the inside corner of her right eye, but refused to fall. Princess Jewel moved closer and rested her hand on the Queen's arm. She seemed to be sharing, and thus easing, Her Majesty's pain.

When the Queen could speak, she said, "Our worlds are almost identical in so many ways; size, climate, geography. Yet our histories have unfolded differently. We have made different moral choices. Yours have caused you untold miseries. We have been spared such catastrophes—until recently. There is growing dissent in First Realm and bloodshed in the Palace of Peace. The King—my father—was murdered."

"I'm sorry," Matterhorn said. "When did this happen?"

"Not long before the Sword called you the first time."

"Did you catch the murderers?" Jewel asked.

"We caught the assassin, but not the traitors. Everyone pays me lip service as Queen, but there are heretics in high places or my father would still be alive."

"Are these the heretics who sent the wraith after Ian's Flute?" Matterhorn asked. He remembered the pirate captain melting into black smoke upon being run through by the Sword of Truth.

"I suspect so," Bea replied.

"What do they want?"

"To take over your world," she said bluntly.

Troubled Realm

IT was dark by now; the fire had burned to dim orange coals. Jewel served mint tea in wooden mugs. The fragrance was soothing in contrast to the Queen's startling words.

"Because your world is so like ours," she explained, "it has attracted great attention. There is growing concern you will destroy yourselves and turn this paradise into a nuclear wasteland. You have come within minutes of doing this several times already."

Bea shifted on her log seat and sipped her tea. "It is against everything we believe to interfere with other races before they have matured," she continued, "but some heretics are calling for direct intervention. Others have gone farther. They are secretly working to write themselves into your future by changing your past. My father strongly opposed them and was killed as a result."

"What can we do to help you?" Jewel asked.

"The role of the Travelers has changed because of something my father did before his death," the Queen replied. "He realized the heretics would need some of the Ten Talis to carry out their plan, so he had the Captain of the Praetorians hide several of them on Earth. The Captain never returned from this mission. The heretics must have followed and murdered him as well, although that would have been a difficult task indeed."

Matterhorn was temporarily distracted when a large rabbit hopped from the bushes and plopped between Jewel's feet. Without taking her eyes off the Queen, Jewel began scratching the furry newcomer's head. Only then did Matterhorn notice the lizard lying by the fish tattoo on her ankle. The Princess seemed to be an animal magnet.

He tuned his mental radio back to Queen Bea and heard, "The Captain left some clues that we have since uncovered. We know he hid the Talis among creatures that are separate from your mainstream history."

"Such as the leprechauns," Matterhorn spoke up. "He hid the Talis in our fairy tales."

"What better place to hide fantastic treasures than in fantasies," Jewel put in.

The Queen smiled at their perceptiveness.

"And you think there's a Talis hidden in an underground city near here?" Matterhorn asked.

"My people have many legends about a secret city," Jewel said. "They say that *Sesqec* once lived there."

"That is true," the Queen said. "They have what I seek."

"What are you talking about?" Matterhorn wanted to know. "*Who* has the Talis?"

Jewel stood to stretch her legs. The Man-in-the-Moon beamed over her right shoulder. Her face was in the shadows but there was no missing the gleam in her eye as she said, "*Sesqec* is the Native American word for Sasquatch. Your people call them Bigfoot."

First leprechauns, Matterhorn thought, now Sasquatch. "So Sasquatch are real," he said to the Queen, who was also standing now.

"Many of the Native American stories about the Sasquatch are true," Bea said. "The legends will help you find the city. When you do, look for this." She bent and retrieved an article from her knapsack. Matterhorn threw more wood on the fire so they could see better.

"This is a replica of the Band of Justice," the Queen said, handing Jewel a circular band of material about an inch wide. Webbed to its smooth white surface with delicate gold filigree was a triangular-faceted ruby. Inscribed around the woven cloth in ruby chips the size of rice grains were these words: *I know in depth your deepest thoughts.*

"The real Band of Justice is made from Morning Cloth," the Queen said. "The Maker cut and set the gem Himself. This Talis represents His all-knowing mind. It allows the wearer to know the thoughts of anyone he or she touches." Bea paused for effect. "Invading someone's inner privacy is never to be done lightly. The Band is used by the King or Queen only when the truth cannot be learned any other way. I need the true Band of Justice to find my father's killers."

Jewel half raised her hand as if she were in school. "If you know where the Talis are hidden, why not go to the exact locations and get them?"

Reaching down for her pack, Queen Bea sighed. "I wish it were that easy. The Captain was careful not to reveal too much in his clues in case the heretics found them. We know to whom he committed some of the Talis, but not the exact times. Also, we must be discrete in searching; there are spies among us. I do not want to repeat my earlier mistake when I went to look for Ian's Flute."

"What mistake?" Matterhorn asked.

"I was gone too long," she said. "Time moves more slowly for those we leave behind when we travel. Still, it does move. Trayko is covering for me, but I must return before I am missed. I do not want to draw attention to your whereabouts."

Matterhorn remembered the tall Praetorian to whom the Baron had introduced him.

Jewel handed the Band back to Bea.

"Keep it," Bea said. "It might come in handy. Be careful, Princess." With that, she motioned for Matterhorn to follow and started uphill toward the cave.

"One more question, please," he said as he caught up. "Does my being here mean I'm an official Traveler?" The Baron had called him one, but Matterhorn wanted to hear the words from the Queen.

She regarded him thoughtfully. "You are something different. A Traveler, certainly, but unique."

"I know it's not my age," Matterhorn replied. "I was told kids are recruited as Travelers. Why is that? Why not use scientists or psychologists to keep an eye on humanity's progress?"

"Because young minds are not yet hardened into categories like 'possible' and 'impossible.' Children are much better at believing than adults. Faith comes naturally to you. Do you know what faith is?" She didn't wait for a response. "It is being certain of what you cannot see. Without faith it is impossible to know the Maker or hear His voice."

They had reached the cave. Queen Bea stopped and stared up into Matterhorn's eyes. "Conduct yourself with courage my brave knight. Find the Talis. Protect the Princess with your life. The Baron will have the supplies you need. Nate the Great may come also, who knows. He travels by his own rules." Standing on her tiptoes, she placed her right hand on his shoulder and squeezed. "Serve well."

"Serve long," Matterhorn replied, returning the salute.

Then the Queen spun on her heels and walked into the cave.

Unexpected Guest

J EWEL had the fire blazing when Matterhorn returned. She sat in the stillness rubbing the rabbit with her bare feet and watching fireflies flit through the trees around the clearing.

Matterhorn resumed his place across from her. He played with the hair behind his left ear and wondered what to do next.

The night crowded closer, its Cyclops-eye watching them from a dark face pimpled with stars. Jewel looked up and said, "I do love being outdoors. It's so, so majestic!"

"You're not frightened being in a strange place?"

"Of what?"

"Well, there might be wild animals around," Matterhorn said.

"Like that grizzly bear?" She glanced to Matterhorn's left.

He spun and searched the gloom for animal eyes. Seeing nothing, he turned on Jewel, expecting a "made you look" remark.

She was serious, yet calm.

"What bear?" he asked.

"The one sitting thirty yards away."

"How do you know?"

"I can smell her for one thing. Also, I have this sixth sense about animals. It's like I can *feel* their feelings. My dad says I'm empathic. Whenever I travel, my senses get sharper. You know how our bodies mature. Well, my animal awareness also becomes more acute."

"Will the bear bother us?" Matterhorn asked nervously.

Jewel laughed. "No, she's just curious about the fire. It's new to her. Is it okay if I invite her over?"

"You can do that?"

"Sure." As Jewel closed her eyes, the rabbit at her feet opened his and a second later bounced into the underbrush. In a few moments Matterhorn could hear the grizzly approaching. A big, black nose on the end of a long, brown snout poked into the firelight. The bear sniffed at the wisps of smoke floating overhead then strutted past Matterhorn and harrumphed down where the bunny had been.

The brute weighed six hundred pounds and measured four feet at the shoulders. Five-inch claws made each paw a formidable weapon. Matterhorn put his hand on the hilt of his Sword. He relaxed somewhat when the blade didn't extend. Evidently they weren't in danger.

Becoming as still as the log on which he sat, Matterhorn gawked as Jewel stood and scratched the bear's neck. She took the stewpot that had been cooling in the dirt and gave it to their guest. The bear's long pink tongue scrubbed it shiny clean.

"I so love animals," Jewel said, burying her fingers deep in the grizzly's coarse fur. "My people have always had a deep respect for all living things; I inherited it from them. My great-grandfather was a famous chief. My dad says that makes me a princess. That's how I got my nickname."

When she finished with the stewpot, the bear pawed at the fire. She quickly dropped the orange coal she had scooped up to examine. After that she gave Matterhorn a good sniffing, which made him sweat despite the night chill. Finally she bestowed a goodnight lick on Jewel and wandered off, leaving behind a steaming memento of her visit.

Matterhorn scooted the scat out of the way with a branch.

Jewel laughed at his fussiness. "Come on," she said. "I'll show you which ferns make the most comfortable sleeping mats."

While they were collecting their feathery bedding, a skittering of rocks sounded from the direction of the cave. Matterhorn's face brightened. "Maybe it's the Baron."

"No, it's the bear," Jewel said. "The Baron doesn't make much noise."

"Have you traveled with him before?"

"A few times. He's one of the best Travelers ever. Did you know that? No one's more trusted by the Praetorians."

Matterhorn wasn't surprised by the Baron's reputation, having seen him in action.

"Those fronds to your left are good," Jewel said. Her own arms were full by now and she headed back to camp where they made beds on opposite sides of the fire circle.

"One time the Baron went after a fellow Traveler who had a mountain climbing accident," Jewel said from across the dying embers. "He found the guy in a blizzard and brought him down, even though the man had a broken leg. This was before he had the Cube, and the rescue took two weeks. They survived on what the Baron had in his pack."

"He's got some amazing gear," Matterhorn agreed. "Most of it he made himself." Matterhorn picked at his teeth with a twig and glanced sideways at his new partner. "The Baron thinks highly of you as a Traveler as well. He was disappointed when you weren't available to help him find Ian's Flute and he got stuck with me."

"From what the Queen told me, you did quite well."

"Beginner's luck," Matterhorn said.

"I don't think so," Jewel replied, "or you would be called Matterhorn the Lucky, not Matterhorn the Brave."

Assuming she was an adolescent like himself and Aaron when not traveling, Matterhorn asked, "How old are you?"

"Thirteen."

"What grade are you in?"

"That depends on the subject. I'm homeschooled because of where I live." She thought for a moment and added, "I suppose I'm mostly in the seventh grade."

"I don't know much about your tribe," Matterhorn admitted.

"Most people don't. The Chinook lived peacefully in the Great Northwest for centuries. After Lewis and Clark arrived with their germs and diseases, we went from being one of the most powerful West Coast tribes to near extinction."

Matterhorn did know enough history to feel ashamed of what his ancestors had done to the Native Americans.

"Some Chinooks ended up on reservations in Washington and Oregon," Jewel went on. "The rest scattered. My family lives in a national park. My dad's a U.S. forest ranger."

"How did you become a Traveler?" Matterhorn asked.

"My grandmother is a healer," Jewel said. "I found out on my tenth birthday that she was also a Traveler in her youth. She told me about her adventures and asked if I wanted to travel. I learned later that this happens a lot. Those with personal experience can often spot others who would make good Travelers."

Jewel leaned up on one elbow. "Several weeks after I said yes, grandmother brought me to the portal you came through this afternoon. It's just a few hours' walk from my house. I met a Praetorian who took me to the Propylon to begin my training."

"Did you meet Queen Bea?"

"Later," Jewel replied, touching the onyx earring Bea had given her. "Only she wasn't a Queen—"

Just then, a tremor rolled through the ground and shook loose a volley of pinecones that peppered the campsite like brown hail.

It was an unsettling omen of things to come.

Morning Briefing

MATTERHORN awoke stiff and cold, but not as chilled as he should have been. During the night he had been covered to conserve his body heat. The shiny space blanket he found on top of him seemed familiar.

"It's 7:15 already; about time you woke up." Warming his hands by a crispy fire sat a bronzed and buzz-cut young man. A red corduroy baseball cap kept the morning sun out of his eyes, which were the color of faded denim. Under his insulated vest he had on a gray T-shirt that stretched across his muscular chest. The pockets of his cargo pants bulged with who-knew-what. Two over-sized backpacks lined with silver tape leaned together a few feet away.

Matterhorn sat up and draped his arms across his knees. "Hey Aaron, great to see you. How've you been?"

"Fine, Matterhorn. And you?"

"No complaints." Noticing that the Baron wore no watch, Matterhorn asked, "How do you know what time it is?"

"Internal clock," the Baron said, tapping his temple. "I always know what time it is."

"When did you get here?"

"An hour ago."

Gazing around the campsite, Matterhorn said, "Where's Jewel?"

"I haven't seen her. She's probably getting breakfast."

"While you two chat the morning away," Jewel said.

The Baron stood as Jewel came through the trees carrying her stewpot brimming with strawberries almost the size of apples.

"Hello, Princess," he said, scooping her into a great hug and swinging her round and round. Strawberries flew everywhere.

Jewel laughed. "Put me down, you brute."

"You must be thinking of someone else," he said, lowering her.

"I'm thinking it's about time you got here," Jewel said.

"I wouldn't have missed this adventure for anything. Especially if you're doing the cooking."

"The Maker made today's breakfast," she said, handing the half-empty pot to the Baron. "Pick up what you spilled and I'll make some tea."

Matterhorn would have preferred hot chocolate but the tea was hot and flavorful. The strawberries tasted sweeter than anything he could remember. He chewed slowly, savoring each bite, and listened as the Baron and Jewel got caught up.

"How's your mom doing?" the Baron asked.

Matterhorn now recalled that Jewel hadn't gone to Ireland with them because her mom was dying of cancer. He felt ashamed at having forgotten such an important detail.

Jewel took a large breath and let it out slowly. "Mom didn't do well with the last round of chemo, so she's stopped going to the clinic. Her older sister—my Aunt Anna—died of cancer two years ago, which scares Dad and me. We're praying for a miracle."

The Baron patted her hand. "I don't know what I'd do if I lost my mom. It must be hard for you to leave her, even for a short time."

"She's at Grandma's for a few weeks," Jewel replied. "Grandma wants to try some herbal treatments. Besides, when I found out this trip was to where my ancestors lived, I couldn't resist." She told Aaron what Bea had said last night about the trouble in First Realm, the missing Talis, the Band of Justice, and the Sasquatch.

The Baron listened quietly, nodding from time to time. "The Queen briefed me about the heretics and the Talis," he said when Jewel finished. "She also said there were clues in the Chinook legends about the Sasquatch."

Jewel topped off their mugs of green tea and said, "I've been thinking about that. The stories tell of a hidden city in a valley somewhere between two fire mountains, which have to be Mount St. Helens and Mount Adams."

Matterhorn scanned the two peaks visible above the treetops. "Both of them are volcanoes," he said.

"And those are just the big ones," the Baron added. "This whole territory is like an underground nuclear test site."

"The Queen said a major earthquake could seal off the city any day now," Jewel went on. "We should get going. Yesterday I spotted the canyon of a large river. It's as good a place as any to start."

"The oracle has spoken," the Baron quipped, wiping strawberry juice from his chin and slurping the last of his tea. He pointed at the packs and said to Matterhorn, "These are much newer than the ones we used in Ireland. I brought you a change of clothes and a pair of lightweight hiking boots. Size thirteen, right?"

"Yeah. How far into the past have we gone?" Matterhorn asked as he dug into the pack.

"To around 10,000 B.C.," the Baron said.

Matterhorn moved a coil of lightweight rope and a flat roll of duct tape to find the boots. Noticing a blue bundle beneath them he asked, "What's this?"

"A small parachute," the Baron answered.

"A parachute! What am I supposed to do with that?"

"The terrain around here is pretty rugged. We might have to drop into a canyon or check out a crater or two." He poked Matterhorn in the side. "Besides, BASE jumping is exciting."

"Extreme sports aren't my style," Matterhorn protested. "The only thing I'm going to use this for is a pillow."

"Stop talking, start walking," Jewel said. She shouldered her own pack, which Matterhorn hadn't noticed before. He scolded himself for not being more observant. Sherlock Holmes would scoff at his inattention to details.

But not even the world's greatest detective would have spotted the keen red eyes watching from the cave as the trio broke camp and headed west. Even Jewel, with her ability to sense the presence of other creatures, was unaware they had company.

Three Faces West

WITH a belly full of sweetness and a heart ready for adventure, Matterhorn followed Jewel and the Baron into the multicolored forest. Blue and purple huckleberries grew among the drooping pink clusters of flowering currant. Blades of yellow sunlight sliced through the leafy canopy overhead and splattered on the ground.

"Do you realize we're in a temperate rainforest?" Jewel asked over her shoulder. "Even in our day this place gets almost fourteen feet of rain a year. That's why it's so lush. I should know; I live here." She led the way through the matted undergrowth of cloverleaf oxalis and blunt sword ferns, jumping over fallen trees with deer-like grace.

They hiked through stands of ponderosa pines and red cedars thicker than bear fur. The Baron and Matterhorn were thankful when Jewel settled on an animal trail that made the going a bit easier. In half an hour they came to a large tear in the earth's skin. The canyon was deeper than it was wide. At its bottom a frisky river could be heard playing among massive boulders.

Shying away from the edge, Matterhorn asked shakily, "Now where?" He had a sinking feeling behind his belly button.

"Down," Jewel said. "This trail goes to the bottom. It's steep, but if animals can use it so can we."

Patting the bottom of his pack, the Baron said, "Or, we can use the parachutes."

Matterhorn didn't like either option. As the Queen's knight he was supposed to be courageous. Hadn't he tackled a gang of pirates? Hadn't he wrestled a wraith? So why couldn't he hike down the side of this canyon?

Acrophobia.

Matterhorn the Brave was afraid of heights. He scratched the hair behind his left ear while his face flushed. How embarrassing not to be able to follow their female guide. "Sorry to make this difficult," he mumbled. "I have this thing about heights."

"That's okay," Jewel said, understanding at once. "We can walk the ridge for a while. Maybe there's a safer way down. No sense taking unnecessary risks."

"The view up here is better anyway," the Baron said, deciding not to tease Matterhorn about his phobia. After all, Matterhorn hadn't made fun of his fear of snakes when they encountered one on their last adventure.

The rest of the morning they tickled the lip of the canyon. A few more downward possibilities came along, but none that Matterhorn could bring himself to take. Along the way they pooled their knowledge about the Sasquatch.

They would have kept their voices down had they known who was listening.

"In my research for this trip," the Baron told his companions, "I read that Sasquatch is an Indian term meaning 'hairy man.' The adults can be nine feet tall and weigh half a ton. They're solitary creatures who have never been seen in groups."

"If they're so solitary," Matterhorn asked, "why are we looking for a whole city of them?"

The Baron shrugged. "Their habits must have changed over the centuries."

"Native Americans regard them with great respect," Jewel said. "We have many tales about our great elder brothers. Some believe they possess both animal and human consciousness. Others say they can sense when people are hunting them. That's why no Sasquatch has ever been killed or captured. It also helps that they're stronger than grizzlies and faster than horses."

"Will they know we mean them no harm?" Matterhorn wondered.

"If they don't figure that out," Jewel said, "we'll never get close enough to find the Band of Justice."

"Finding the Talis won't be easy," the Baron said. "Did the Queen mention Nate?"

"She said he might show up; she wasn't sure," Matterhorn replied.

"We could use his help. That bushman could track a polar bear in a blizzard."

They walked and talked for several more hours. At one point Jewel climbed alone to the top of a ridge where a buck and two does were nibbling bushes. When she came back she announced, "There's a river not far ahead that cuts a gentler path to the canyon floor. We can follow it down."

"The deer told you that!" Matterhorn said in amazement.

"No," Jewel said. "I could see it from the high ground."

The lazy tributary took its own sweet time yielding to gravity. It preferred to double back on itself rather than risk steep drops. Following the winding water and using the dense vegetation as handholds, the Travelers made it to the bottom by sundown. The river noise made it difficult to carry on a conversation, which didn't matter since everyone was talked out. Exhausted from their trek, they didn't bother with a fire.

The Baron dug out three MREs—meals ready to eat. He cut the large plastic casing in which they were issued and dumped out the contents: chicken-and-rice main course, crackers, cheese spread with jalapenos, fudge brownie, Skittles, cherry-flavored beverage powder, and a baggie of spices. He showed Matterhorn and Jewel how to slide the meal pouch into the green sleeve with a chemical heating wafer. The result wasn't gourmet, but it was hot and filling.

They spent the night on moss-covered ground that smelled of humus and awoke before the sun could haul its round bottom over the canyon rim. Jewel scrounged for fruit and nuts while the Baron started a fire.

"We should head downriver," Jewel said, as she brewed her morning tea, "not upriver like we discussed last night."

"Why the change?" Matterhorn asked.

"The canyon narrows upstream. Downstream looks more promising."

She must have been up for hours to have scouted both directions, Matterhorn realized. He felt guilty for sleeping in.

Jewel and the Baron let Matterhorn take the point this morning. Even he could follow a stream. This particular one was on its way to make a deposit of melted snow in the Pacific. The atmosphere above was crisp and clean, thanks to a vigorous routine of daily showers. The rocky walls were serrated on top and studded with trees that grew wherever a few inches of dirt had collected over the ages.

Hawks circled on updrafts. Deer and elk signs littered the canyon floor as it widened. A set of fresh tracks in the soft earth caught Matterhorn's attention. He knelt and studied the prints. "Keep your eye peeled for a large wolf," he said. "These paw prints are huge."

Jewel smiled but said nothing.

At one o'clock they reached a fork in the river. Jewel suggested the left prong—and regretted it two hours later. The banks on both sides of the chasm had narrowed and then disappeared in the spray of churning rapids.

They would have to shoot Class V white water or turn back.

U-turn

WE could make a raft and keep going!" the Baron yelled as they rested on a granite slab not far from the mouth of the cataract. "I've got some rope; there's enough fallen birch around."

Matterhorn snapped a branch off a downed tree. "How are we supposed to trim these trees into logs?"

"With a wire saw!" the Baron said. "There's one in your pack!" From his own gear he pulled out a small loop of flexible black-oxide-coated wire. The twenty-four-inch strand had ring handles on either end. "These babies will zip through wood, metal, bone—you name it!" As he spoke, he deftly trimmed one side of the log on the ground between them.

"A raft might work if the rapids don't go on too long!" Jewel said, cupping her hands to her mouth. "That chop will shred it otherwise!"

"I'm good with knots!" the Baron cried, rolling the log over with his foot and starting on the other side.

"The SS *Princess* will hold together and get us through, captain!" He gave Jewel a military salute.

Jewel tossed one of the severed branches into the stream and watched it vanish into the swirling vortex. "Have you ever played Rock, Paper, Scissors?" she asked. "Well, in Rock, Rapids, Raft. Raft loses!"

"Speaking of losing!" the Baron countered, "we'll lose too much time if we have to backtrack!"

"Better than losing our lives!"

"Do you think the Maker would let that happen?"

"Do you think He will protect us from our own stupidity?"

Matterhorn interrupted the squabbling, "Jewel has a point!" he yelled at the Baron. "We have no idea what's ahead!"

Jewel shielded her eyes with a hand and studied the terrain. Finding what she wanted, she scampered uphill to a towering Sitka spruce. She kicked off her moccasins and climbed out of sight like a long-haired squirrel. Ten minutes later she was down with news that the narrows got much worse beyond these first rocks.

"Forget a raft!" she insisted. "I wouldn't go in there on a submarine!" She scooped up her pack and started upstream.

By the time they backtracked to the fork, darkness was already pouring over the sides of the gorge like spilled ink. They would have to wait till tomorrow to explore the other branch of the stream. With nothing to show for the day's effort but sore feet, Matterhorn,

Jewel, and the Baron settled for another night in the canyon. They camped in a broad meadow far enough from the water to be able to converse without yelling.

Jewel found a secluded pool where they took turns washing up. It was the coldest, and shortest, bath Matterhorn had ever taken. They fished for supper and feasted on brookies. After dinner, Matterhorn asked to see the copy of the Band of Justice. "If this is a fake, the original must really be something."

"I think the ruby is real," Jewel said. "I've never seen a gem that big. It must be worth a mint."

Matterhorn was more interested in the inscription. He compared it with the writing on the crosspiece of his Sword. Both matched the script he had seen on Ian's Flute. Assuming each Talis had been inscribed by its creator, he asked the Baron, "What's written on the Traveler's Cube?"

Aaron tossed the Talis to Matterhorn. "See if you can find it."

Returning the Band to Jewel, he held the Cube close to the fire. The alien object reminded him of a warped Rubik's cube. The twisted ball was a mosaic of flat gemstones seamlessly welded together. The surface shifted under his touch as if the ball was full of thick jelly. He had a severe case of eyestrain by the time he found the thin blue line threading among the gems.

The barely legible writing read: *I am Beginning, End, and all Between*. "The inscriptions are in English," Matterhorn noted.

"They're in whatever language the reader knows," the Baron replied.

"What aspect of the Maker does the Cube represent?" Matterhorn asked.

"His omnipresence. The fact that He's everywhere all at once. There's no place we can go where He isn't."

"Who had the Cube before Queen Bea gave it to you?"

"The Praetorians," the Baron replied. "They used it to open new portals."

Fingering the fantastic device, Matterhorn got a flash of inspiration. "Why not use this to go back in time and ask the Captain of the Praetorians where he hid the Talis? Better still, have him give them to you!"

Matterhorn was disappointed that the Baron didn't share his excitement. "You could even go back and warn the king of First Realm of the assassination plot!" Matterhorn added. "Bea wouldn't have to lose her father!"

The Baron shook his head. "If only it were that easy. I suggested the same ideas after my first trip with the Cube. That's when I learned that Realm time is absolute."

"There's no such thing," Matterhorn said. "Einstein showed that time is relative."

"Einstein never visited First Realm," the Baron replied. "There's no going back there, no revisiting or changing the past."

Jewel wanted to see the Cube next. "How many trips have you taken with this?"

"Quite a few," the Baron said, "but only when I can't use a fixed portal. The Cube consumes a lot of energy and takes time to recharge."

Looking at the shiny strips on their packs, Matterhorn asked, "Is it solar powered?"

"No. The power source is in its core. Probably some form of quantum energy transfer. I've been ordered not to take it apart to find out."

"Why do guys want to dismantle everything?" Jewel said.

"Curiosity."

"Isn't that what killed the cat?"

"Only cats that aren't careful."

"I'm all for curiosity," Jewel said in self-defense. "None of us would be Travelers if we weren't curious. But there's also such a thing as common sense. And taking apart one of the Ten Talis isn't sensible."

The Baron laughed. "The Talis are indestructible. The worst I could do is get it out of alignment."

"Is it worth the risk?"

"I'm trying to learn how it works. That knowledge may come in handy someday."

"Or get you stranded somewhere."

Moose Meadow

ALL the next morning they kept moving west until the canyon walls finally petered out. The terrain opened up and by early afternoon the Travelers found themselves on a gently sloping plateau. Warm grass engulfed their legs and Matterhorn felt like he was wading in a shallow green swamp.

A flock of birds feeding on some scraggly bushes caught Jewel's attention. She went to investigate and returned with a shirttail full of sour berries for lunch.

"Are you sure these are safe?" the Baron asked through puckered lips.

"Most black or blue berries are edible," Jewel said. "Red berries are riskier. White berries are almost always poisonous."

"What do you eat when berries aren't in season?" Matterhorn wanted to know.

"If you are desperate, you can eat the birds. All species are edible."

"Especially chicken and turkey," the Baron said. "With a side of mashed potatoes and gravy. Mmm."

A bull moose bellowed at them from a stand of trees. The hump on his back loomed up between the sides of his five-foot rack. His shoulders bulged outward from a thick neck that supported a long, ugly head.

Whistling in awe, Matterhorn said, "Now I know what 'big as a moose' means. He's enormous."

"They're the largest members of the deer family in North America," Jewel said. "A bull like that can weigh up to 1,200 pounds. He's warning us to stay out of his meadow. See how his ears are laid back and his hump is arched."

"A wide berth it is," the Baron said, getting up to leave. "I got chased by a moose once in Alaska. They're much faster than they look."

"They can charge at thirty miles an hour," Jewel said.

"You've had experience with them?" the Baron asked.

"Some. They're not the brightest beasts in the forest, but they're good-natured, as long as you don't come between a cow and her calf."

"Which is exactly what we did."

"Who's 'we'?" Matterhorn asked. "And what were you doing in Alaska?"

"My uncle Shaun took me there for my twelfth birthday," the Baron replied. "Sort of a 'rites of passage' deal. We spent two weeks in Denali National Park." The Baron's face brightened with the memory. "He's a fireman now but he used to be a PJ."

"Your uncle used to be a pair of pajamas?" Matterhorn teased.

"He was an Air Force Para-Jumper," the Baron said,
unimpressed by Matterhorn's attempt at humor. "They're
the most highly trained search and rescue forces in the
world. Anyway, we had a great time. He taught me all
sorts of survival skills."

"Which one did you use to escape the moose?" Jewel
asked.

The Baron put both hands on the base of his spine
and stretched his back. "Tell me what you would have
done."

"I wouldn't have walked between a cow and her
young," Jewel said.

"A white man's mistake," Aaron admitted.

"If attacked," Jewel said, "I would drop to the
ground, curl into a ball and pretend to be a rock. Moose
are color-blind; if you don't move they can't see you."

"I did the exact opposite," the Baron said. "I was so
scared I bolted. My uncle kept his head, though. He
grabbed a rotting branch off the ground and smacked it
into a tree. It sounded like a gun shot and distracted the
moose long enough for me to climb a tree."

It started to drizzle so the hikers put on their pon-
chos. Soon real raindrops were splattering them and glaz-
ing the grass. They moved closer to the river, which
didn't need this added encouragement as it picked up
speed on the slight incline.

Matterhorn wiped rain and sweat from his steamy
face. A half mile away he could see where the highland

ended as abruptly as a table. He could faintly hear the water barreling over the edge. "So much for following the river," he said to Jewel.

"We'll have to find another—" An ominous thunderclap cut her off as the weather took a rude turn. The rain plops hardened to pellets fired from a shotgun gray sky. The stinging barrage of hail left Matterhorn unsure of what to do. He didn't like getting blasted, but he had been taught to avoid trees during a storm.

Not far ahead a compromise presented itself in a stand of pines on the riverbank. Jewel pointed out a stunted tree on its fringe, more of a bush than a tree. Being shorter than its neighbors, it was a less likely target for lightning. Its splayed branches would provide at least some protection and she led the others toward it.

Just as they reached the pines, the earth joined the sky in objecting to these trespassers being here before their time. It gave a sudden, massive shudder and everything shifted sideways. The trees cracked heads. The river sloshed out of its bed. The humans went sprawling.

The Baron grabbed for a branch.

Matterhorn grabbed for the Baron.

Jewel grabbed for Matterhorn—and missed!

She slid down the bank and into the rushing stream as helpless as a flipped turtle.

Raging River

WHEN the earth stopped shaking, Matterhorn struggled to his feet and went after Jewel. The Baron had already rolled out of his pack and was sprinting downriver. He managed to shed his poncho and kick off his boots while gaining on the Princess.

Matterhorn had no idea the Baron could run so fast. Neither did the Baron. But a friend's life was at stake. He caught up with Jewel and dove into the torrent. Ice water rushed up his nose and froze his sinuses. He spat out muddy gulps of foam as he swam furiously toward the thrashing figure. Wet clothes tangled around his limbs, which soon became stiff with cold. The noise of the waterfall ahead filled him with dread, but he blocked out the sound and concentrated on reaching Jewel.

By the time he got to her, she had stopped moving. He flipped her over and kept her head above water. But with his arms full, he had only his legs to propel them back to shore.

It wouldn't be enough.

He had used every ounce of energy to get this far and strained every muscle to the limit. His legs had turned to foam rubber. His burning lungs couldn't get enough air. If only Jewel could help, but she was unconscious. The turbulence pounded them. Icy fingers clawed at their skin.

While his body strained against the inevitable, the Baron's mind went strangely calm. So this is what it feels like to die, he thought as he sped with his lifeless burden toward the end of the plateau. He would never see his mother again. Throw a baseball. Watch a movie. Joke around with Matterhorn. A quiet sadness closed over him; he prepared to meet his Maker.

Back on shore, Matterhorn charged through the buckshot rain, straining to catch up. He realized he would lose the race to the cliff. The current, swollen by snowmelt, was too swift, the edge too close. His friends were going to die and he couldn't prevent it. Fear squeezed his chest and congealed his blood to jelly.

No longer careful of his footing, he slipped on the rocks. Scrambling to his feet, he stumbled on. How could the Baron and Jewel die like this? What about their calling as Travelers? Where was the Maker when they needed Him most?

Matterhorn screamed into the dark sky, "Help us!"

Amidst the surrounding chaos, he heard a voice that had spoken to him when his own life had been in peril. It spoke the word that could save the Baron and Jewel, and Matterhorn began yelling that word with all his might!

"SARA!"

He cupped his hands around his mouth and screamed over and over as he ran.

"SARA! SARA! SARA!"

Above the din of the stream, the Baron heard Matterhorn's shouts. What was he yelling?

Sir?

Air?

Sara!

SARA!

Why hadn't he thought of her before! The Baron let go of Jewel with one hand and fished the vial from his thigh pocket. He yanked the stopper out with chattering teeth. A fine mist rose and became the most gorgeous woman he had ever seen. And what made Sara especially beautiful at this moment was her ability to do wondrous things with water.

The revived water nymph took in the situation. Although she had been in the vial for a long time, to her only a second had passed since she'd been speaking with Queen Bea on the Irish coast. Her Majesty had commanded the Baron to take Sara with him. It was a good thing for the human that he had obeyed.

Sara diverted the rushing water to one side of the Baron and Jewel while she pushed their bodies toward land. She also made the water around them bubble with oxygen to keep them afloat. By the time the half-drowned couple drew near enough to shore that Matterhorn could haul them to safety, they were less than fifty yards from the edge of the plateau.

The Baron was exhausted, but waved off any help. Jewel needed CPR, which Matterhorn applied, thankful for what he'd learned at swimming lessons.

After coughing up a chest-full of water, Jewel sputtered weakly, "What a ride." She rolled her head to the side and saw the Baron lying nearby, his clothes soaked and his skin pale. "Thanks," she mouthed.

The Baron smiled feebly and gave her a thumbs-up.

Glancing above her to where Sara hovered, Jewel blinked several times. Each time her vision refocused, Sara was still there. Befuddled, Jewel said, "I must have hit my head; I'm seeing things."

"I'm not a thing," the water nymph said. "My name is Sara. I'm from Ireland."

"How did you get here?"

"I came in this," Sara replied, holding up the vial the Baron had dropped in the river. Her bright blue eyes twinkled in her doll-like face. A gray shift draped her petite figure, leaving her arms and legs bare.

"I'll explain it to you later," Matterhorn said, patting Jewel's arm. To Sara he said, "Good to see you again. You're a lifesaver."

"That's my line," the Baron rasped. "Sara, I take back what I said about your traveling with us being a bad idea."

Sara giggled like a mountain spring. "Let's see about getting everyone dry." She dissolved upward and a few moments later the rain stopped. Ten minutes later she reappeared. "What a delightful country!" she announced.

"The forest is so much thicker than in Ireland. And it's so *humid*!" She flung her arms wide and twirled like a ballerina.

Matterhorn moved Jewel and the Baron away from the river before going to retrieve their packs. He set up camp in a glade, but had difficulty finding dry kindling and branches to make a fire. Then he hit on the idea of asking Sara to dry the wood, which she did before sailing off to explore this new wonderland. Soon the Travelers were sharing a toasty blaze. The sun shooed away the spent clouds. Birds opened their beaks without fear of drowning, and the forest once more trilled with music.

The Baron got dry but couldn't get warm. His teeth were chattering so hard he couldn't speak.

"You need some medicine and hot food," Jewel said. She wobbled to her feet and told Matterhorn, "Tend the fire; I'm going shopping."

Special Delivery

MATTERHORN did what he could to make the Baron comfortable. He put a pot of water on the fire and collected ferns to dry out for bedding.

The Baron thought about the last time he had been this sick. It was a few summers ago, which meant he was at his grandparents. His time at the ranch was the best part of every year. True, he had had a few medical emergencies there, but the good memories far out-weighed the bad.

His grandpa was the closest thing to a father in his life. His real dad had walked out when Aaron was three. Before taking early retirement and buying the 3,000-acre spread, grandpa had been an engineer. He converted one of the barns into a world-class workshop and loved to tinker with everything from computers to hay balers. It was in this magical place that Aaron discovered his love of machines and his flare for invention.

The Baron didn't have the energy to share his memories with Matterhorn. Instead he curled up and tried to sleep. He woke up when Jewel returned. She fixed a supper of tossed greens and wood sorrel soup, flavored with venison jerky from her pack. Plump blackberries did a fine impersonation of dessert. But all that the Baron managed to get down were a few sips of broth.

Jewel feared he might have pneumonia.

His shivering got worse after sundown. Even under the space blanket he couldn't keep warm. Matterhorn extended the blade of his Sword and placed it under the blanket. Recalling what he had done in Ireland, he willed the blade to heat up. He didn't understand the link between his mind and the Talis, but the longer he carried it, the more confident he felt using it.

After the Baron was settled, Matterhorn dried out his quote book and harmonica. Then he lay down and played lullabies. The music calmed his nerves, which were still raw from the day's events. If his friends had gone over the falls, what would have happened to him? He didn't know how to work the portal to get home. He wasn't even sure he could find it again.

Mother Earth hiccupped a few more times that night, but the sleepers were too exhausted to notice. The tremors were a sure sign of more trouble ahead. The Big One was coming.

Shortly after dawn, Jewel woke Matterhorn from a troubled sleep. Worry creased her pretty face. "The Baron is getting worse," she said. "This morning I thought of something that might help. If I can find some mountain mint, I can brew a fever-breaking tea."

"I'm going with you this time," Matterhorn insisted. "Four eyes are better than two."

Jewel didn't argue. She made the Baron as comfortable as possible and whispered in his ear, "We won't be gone long. We'll bring back something to make you better."

Matterhorn didn't have Jewel's skill with animals and he dreaded going into the wilderness unarmed. Yet if he took his Sword he would be depriving the Baron of its warmth.

Seeing Matterhorn's concern, the Baron said, "Take my switchwhip."

"Thanks." Matterhorn pulled the smooth stick from its narrow pocket on the Baron's leg. The press of a button on the weapon would release an eight-foot leather lash with a poisoned tip.

Jewel described what they were looking for as they left camp.

"Where did you learn about plants?" Matterhorn asked.

"My grandmother has been teaching me the medicinal benefits of plants and herbs. For hundreds of years my people have been filling our prescriptions at nature's pharmacy. Many modern drugs are based on natural remedies." To illustrate, she pointed out the scarlet fruit of devil's club and the single nodding flower of Indian pipe and described their curative powers.

Matterhorn would have been more interested in the lecture if he wasn't so focused on finding a single stalk of mountain mint, which they never did.

Jewel peeled a chunk of bark off a willow tree and said, "At least this is better than nothing."

"What's in that?"

"Salicylic acid." When Matterhorn's face remained blank, she added, "Aspirin."

Back at camp the Baron was getting worse. He had dosed himself with penicillin from his first-aid kit, but it hadn't helped. The chill burrowed deeper into his bones. He hated feeling this weak and vulnerable and his thoughts turned homeward. With a twist of his Cube he could be there. He could rest in his own bed and let his mom fill him with homemade chicken noodle soup when she got home from work.

Aaron loved the excitement of being a Traveler and of having contact with First Realm. He got an adult body and the ability to journey through time and see the world. The job used to involve observing and reporting, but since the death of the King and the undeclared war for the Talis, it had become much more dangerous. The great privilege now carried greater peril.

As in any conflict, there would be casualities. Continued service to the Maker would include hardship, perhaps even death. Hadn't he and Matterhorn come within a whisker of being killed over Ian's Flute?

His mood grew more somber, yet in the end he decided to stick it out with Matterhorn and Jewel. They wouldn't quit or slink home and neither would he. He dozed fitfully, only to be awakened by bouts of uncontrollable coughing.

Around noon, Matterhorn and Jewel returned and found the Baron asleep. Everything appeared as they had left it—except for the stalks of mountain mint spread out to dry on rocks near the freshly stoked fire.

Matterhorn awoke Aaron and asked about the plants. The Baron had no idea how they had gotten there. Ignoring the mystery for the moment, Jewel put some water on to boil; then set about stripping the downy, lance-pointed leaves from their square stalks. She sang over the leaves as she shredded them, mingling her sweet voice with the fresh fragrance. She also thought to add some lemon balm from her supply of herbs. The Baron forced down almost a cup of the steaming liquid before falling back to sleep.

In the meantime Matterhorn searched the campsite for clues to the identity of their unknown benefactor. Footprints, broken branches, bent ferns, disturbed moss, anything.

Nothing.

Jewel wandered off and eventually came back shaking her head. "None of the nearby wildlife seem out of sorts," she said. "We're the only strangers that have raised their curiosity."

Over a late lunch they traded theories. "Someone knew the exact plant we needed and where to find it," Matterhorn pointed out. "But there aren't any humans around yet. So that only leaves—"

Leap of Faith

S O the Bigfoot know we're here," Matterhorn said to Jewel as he fidgeted with the pile of kindling at his feet. "Does that mean they know what we're after?"

"Maybe," she replied. She was busy grinding the willow bark to red powder. "Some tribes like the Hopi and the Lakota believe Sasquatch have psychic powers. They think they have medicine that makes them invisible when they want to be. The Chinook believe Sasquatch are just physical beings like humans and animals."

As the day wore on, the mint tea laced with aspirin worked its herbal magic. The Baron's eyes became more blue than gray and his fever broke. He was awake and alert for supper, and Matterhorn brought him up to speed while they ate.

"It's obvious the Sasquatch know where *we* are," Aaron agreed. "But they don't want us to know where *they* are. There's nothing to do but keep searching for the city." To Jewel he said, "What else can you tell us about the place from the legends?"

"The entrance is supposed to be shrouded in a rainbow and guarded by the god of thunder."

"That's rather mysterious."

Jewel shrugged. "It's the best I can do. Now drink your tea and be quiet. Save your strength for tomorrow; you'll need it. We have to get moving before the next earthquake hits."

"What kind of bedside manner is that?" the Baron said. He emptied his mug and lay back down.

The next thing he knew it was bright blue morning. Sunshine filled the uncluttered sky and bleached the day moon's already pale face. Moss on white birch and weeping willows made them look like old women draped in wet shawls.

The Baron's melancholy and chill had gone and he felt 80 percent better. Time to get on with the task of finding the Talis. He sat up and scratched his stubble.

"You're starting to look like your old self," Matterhorn said from across the fire. "I guess some things can't be helped." Lofting the switchwhip to the Baron, he added, "Time to trade back." He missed his Sword.

After a breakfast of fruit and nuts, the trio walked the short distance to the edge of the plateau. The forest grew thin as a receding hairline as Jewel led them onto a massive forehead of bare granite. Eight hundred feet below, she and the Baron saw the oval pool into which the waterfall splattered.

Matterhorn had no interest in the view. He was frantically thinking of how to get off this high ground.

"It's awesome!" Jewel yelled at the Baron over the thunderous noise.

The Baron didn't answer. He was staring down at the colorful halo the sun painted on the spray above the large pool. He had never seen a round rainbow before. He signaled Jewel and they rejoined Matterhorn a safe distance from the cliff.

"A rainbow and thunder," the Baron said. "I think we've found the front door to Sasquatch City. And I have just the thing to get us down off the roof." He pulled two silk bundles from his gear and handed one to Jewel. "I knew these would come in handy."

"You're crazy!" Matterhorn cried, taking a few steps backward.

"Are we high enough?" Jewel asked casually as she studied the super lightweight harness.

"High enough!" Matterhorn was beside himself. "You're crazy, too! How can you hang your life by a few threads of silk? My pajamas weigh more than these parachutes!"

"I'm trusting in more than the equipment," Jewel said. "The Maker will get us down."

"Gravity will get us down!" Matterhorn cried. "It's the landing that concerns me!"

"Don't worry," the Baron tried to assure him. "You'll be fine."

His breezy confidence irked Matterhorn. "How do you know? Have you ever done this before?"

"Yes."

That caught Matterhorn by surprise. "Your mom lets you jump off cliffs?" he said in disbelief.

"She doesn't know I jump off cliffs, or scuba dive, or snow camp. She doesn't know I've had survival training or search-and-rescue experience."

"How could she *not* know?"

The Baron cast an impatient look at Matterhorn as if the answer was obvious. "Because I do them when traveling, which is a *secret* occupation. I can't exactly get her to sign a permission slip."

Matterhorn took out his own parachute and fingered the harness straps. "Where'd you get this fancy gear?" he asked.

"Are you curious or just stalling?"

"Both," Matterhorn admitted.

"Tell you what," Aaron said in a sympathetic tone, "I'll explain it to you tonight. Right now we need to get down from here. A slight tremor just then emphasized his point. Who knew how much longer they had before the promised earthquake would make their mission impossible.

Matterhorn spread his feet to keep balance. The Baron was right. They had to do something. Any way off this plateau would be torturous. Might as well get it over with. "If we gotta jump, we gotta jump," he concluded. "Show me how this rig works."

"Shift your pack to the front and put your harness on like so," the Baron began his show-and-tell explanation. "Make sure the straps are tight. This is your pilot chute: hold it in your hand and release it as soon as you clear the cliff. It will pull out your main chute, which will blossom into two hundred square feet of silk. These are your brake lines; make sure they stay outside the keeper rings on the risers . . ."

The instructions lasted a few more minutes and ended with a warning. "The most important thing is to jump far enough from the ledge so you don't hit anything on the way down. You'll be dropping at seventeen feet per second, so you'll have about a fifty-second ride." Showing them once more how to steer by pulling the guidelines, the Baron concluded by saying, "Aim for the water. It will feel better than landing on top of a tree."

"Fifty seconds is way too long," Matterhorn lamented. "Would it go faster if I put rocks in my pocket?"

The Baron's laugh resounded above the falls. "Your pack provides plenty of extra weight. Release your harness when you hit the water so you don't get tangled in the lines. If you need to, you can inflate your pack lining to keep from sinking." He pointed to the tab on the pack's yellow backing.

"Are you two done yapping?" Jewel said. "This eagle's ready to soar!"

The phrase reminded Matterhorn that mother eagles pushed their young out when the time came to leave the nest. No practice runs. No safety nets. No do-overs. Eaglets had to fly or die. He had the same options, only he felt more like a chicken than an eagle.

Jewel retreated several yards. When the Baron gave her a thumbs-up, she zoomed toward the cliff with a yell that would have made Geronimo proud, even though he was an Apache and she was a Chinook.

"You're next," the Baron said. "Remember that you carry the Sword of Truth. It will protect you."

Matterhorn decided that was enough truth on which to take a leap of faith. If he couldn't trust the Maker to preserve his life, he had no business with His Sword. Once more he realized that bravery was not the absence of fear, but the determination to overcome it. He checked his harness while walking to where Jewel had begun her takeoff. Clutching his pilot chute in one white-knuckled hand, he gave the okay signal with the other.

The Baron waved him on. Without another thought Matterhorn began pumping his strong legs toward open sky. No matter how fast they churned they couldn't keep up with his speeding heart. As he shot past the Baron and long-jumped into space he heard, "Serve well!"

To which he shouted with fervent hope, "Serve looooooooong!"

Water Landing

MATTERHORN wanted to close his eyes during his descent, but they were frozen open in fear and wonder. As he sailed over the edge, the wet updraft slapped him in the face and ripped the pilot chute from his grasp. A few seconds later, the main chute jerked him upright with a force that threatened to dislocate his shoulders.

What the Baron saw from the ledge—and what he never mentioned afterward—was how close Matterhorn had come to whacking his head on an outcrop before the parachute opened. The silk actually brushed the rock, but slid off without catching or tearing.

Hanging suspended in space, Matterhorn took his first breath since the jump—a deep, ragged gasp. The spray from the falls drenched him. It felt like he was swimming to earth instead of falling. Between his feet he saw Jewel's yellow-and-red canopy coasting toward the pool. Circles of green surrounded the blue bulls-eye, which grew larger as he watched. He remembered his guidelines and pulled the left one, then the right, struggling to keep sight of Jewel.

He heard the Baron's exuberant laughter from somewhere overhead. The guy was having way too much fun. Matterhorn had to admit the feeling of floating was exhilarating. The drag on his canopy offset the relentless tug of gravity just enough to create a sense of serenity. He even imagined doing this again—in another thousand years or so. The leap off the cliff hadn't killed him. The opening of the chute hadn't torn his arms off. That left him free to worry about the splashdown. He focused on Jewel and tried to copy her movements. At the last second she jerked hard on the right side of her canopy and swerved to a stand-up landing on a slim ribbon of ground by the pool.

"Sweet move!" Matterhorn yelled down. He was still trying to figure out how to duplicate it when he hit the water. The impact stunned him from feet to brain. His pack pulled him under and he got snarled in the guidelines as the turbulence twisted him round and round. Precious seconds struggled by, each one taking a piece of his life. He couldn't wiggle free of his harness and his petrified fingers couldn't find the tab on his pack. He gritted his teeth and prepared to suck air through them as if they were gills.

I can't die, he reminded himself. Not while I have the Sword of Truth on me. But did he still have it, or had it been torn off in this maelstrom? If the Sword was lost, could he still count on being saved? His survival might depend as much on the Baron's scritch pad as on the Maker's Sword.

Neither, it turned out, failed him. The hilt was still on his hip. He yanked it loose, extended the blade halfway and slashed at the tangled lines. The spot of yellow on the edge of his vision turned out to be the tab on the pack liner. He managed to pull it with the last of his fleeting strength. The yellow bladder inflated and hauled him to the surface.

After several gulps of air, Matterhorn expected the grayness in his vision to clear. It didn't. He was floating in a murky world whose only light seeped through a wall of water to his left.

He had landed in broad daylight in front of the falls, but had risen in the gloom behind them. When his eyes adjusted, he could make out a stone anteroom about ten feet high, forty feet long, and twenty feet across. Roots grew down from the ceiling like albino serpents. The walls were slimed with mucus-green moss and lichen. Dog-paddling to the edge, Matterhorn crawled out onto the chamber's stone floor. He heated his Sword and huddled over it in an attempt to get warm.

On the opposite side of the waterfall the Baron had landed next to Jewel. Together they looked for the silk lily pad of Matterhorn's parachute.

"There!" Jewel yelled as the blue fabric bubbled up from beneath the falls.

Still feeling the effects of the pneumonia, the Baron responded sluggishly. Jewel swam out and grabbed the chute and Aaron helped drag it to shore. It was remarkably light.

Too light.

"Something's wrong!" the Baron cried, pulling the parachute hand over hand until he held the severed lines. He scoured the frothing pool for signs of the yellow airbag or Matterhorn's red hair. Seeing nothing, he began to slip off his pack to go in after his friend when Jewel stopped him. She grabbed his shoulders and pushed him toward the bank.

"You're too weak!" she shouted over the din of crashing water. "If the undertow has Matterhorn, you'll never be able to pry him loose! Where's Sara?"

The water nymph had been exploring her new surroundings since being freed from the vial the day before. She had checked on the humans occasionally and had been close by when they jumped from the cliff. On a whim she had decided to follow them down. She needed no artificial help, but simply dove into the stream and tumbled over the edge like a kid on a water slide. Then she floated back to the top in the mist and cascaded down again.

She was so busy playing that she never heard the frantic calls for help.

Open Sesame

T HE Baron was the first to notice the slivers of unnatural light leaking around both sides of the waterfall. It dawned on him that the brilliance could only be coming from one source—the Sword of Truth. He clutched Jewel's arm and shouted, "Matterhorn's behind the falls!"

"I see it!" Jewel cried. "How do we get back there?"

"We'll find a way!" The Baron didn't take time to repack his chute, but shucked out of it and let it float away. Jewel did likewise. This broke one of the rules of traveling—you pack it in, you pack it out—but they had no choice. The fabric would rot long before humans reached this area anyway. Still, he might have some explaining to do if the Queen found out. He began picking his way around the pool's rocky lip.

Jewel took off her moccasins and followed. Years of running barefoot through the woods had hardened her feet. This way she could use her toes to grip the slimy stones. "I saw no signs of a hidden city on the way down!" she hollered as they approached the falls. "Did you?"

"No! But Matterhorn may have stumbled onto what we're looking for!" Pointing ahead he yelled, "What a great place to hide a secret entrance!" A narrow rock ledge cut between a wall of granite and a wall of water. The Baron and Jewel squeezed through the slit and into the Sword-lit cavity.

"I thought you said to land in the water!" Matterhorn yelled at his friends. He sat Indian-style at the far end of the room, the glow of his blade drenching the chamber. "Am I the only one who knows how to follow instructions?"

"I also told you to be careful!" the Baron shouted back. "What about that part?"

"Jumping wasn't my idea in the first place!"

"Stop arguing you two!" Jewel scolded with a smile. She reached Matterhorn first and asked, "Is anything broken?"

"I don't think so!"

Before Aaron could join them, Sara materialized next to him. "You three can't seem to stay out of the water!" she said in her lilting voice. She had finished frolicking and decided to look in on the solid-bodies. Since her unplanned appearance at the river, she had changed her dull gray shift into a silvery sundress. As was her custom, she accented her outfit with local gems. Her jewelry for today—pinky ring, bracelet, pendant, earrings, and ankle bracelet—featured brilliant orange red garnets.

The reunited adventurers sat in a circle and discussed their situation. "The entrance to the city has to be in here somewhere!" the Baron shouted over the water's roar. "Mind if I use this?" he asked, reaching for the Sword.

Matterhorn handed over the Talis and watched the Baron approach the back wall. He began scrambling through the wet greenery until the bright light and sudden commotion dislodged a family of bats. The leathery creatures swooped away in a huff, startling the human intruders. The Baron slipped and stuck out his hand to keep from smashing his face into the rocks.

His hand disappeared into the foliage, followed by his arm, and then his whole body.

The curtain of secrecy had been parted.

Aaron's smiling face popped out a moment later draped in a wig of soggy green dreadlocks. "Spelunking, anyone!" he beamed.

They cleared the camouflage from the cave opening, which turned out to be a ten-foot semicircle that reminded Matterhorn of a giant cartoon mouse hole. The interior was blacker than day-old coffee.

"Let's get inside!" the Baron yelled.

Jewel balked at the suggestion. "Now it's my turn to be scared! Do we have to go in there! It looks like a narrow grave! I can't stand closed-in places!"

"You can do it, Jewel!" the Baron encouraged. "The hidden city might be at the other end of this tunnel."

So in she went, heart beating in her throat and hands shaking in her pockets.

When they were far enough underground to dampen the water noise, the Baron called a halt. He took three baseball caps from his pack-of-plenty, switching one for his red corduroy cap and giving the others to Matterhorn and Jewel. Silver foil lined the inside of each cap. A thin piece of unbreakable glass about two inches in diameter perched above the bills.

The disc on the Baron's cap began to glow as he explained the headgear. "Most of our body heat radiates out of our heads. That's why hats help keep us warm. But these babies aren't designed for warmth. The lining captures one form of energy—heat—and converts it to another form—light."

Matterhorn looked at the Baron's light, which wasn't getting any brighter. "You're a pretty cool head," he quipped. "Are you sure your hat isn't reading brain wave activity?"

"Very funny. I know the lumens aren't much; that's why we also have these." The Baron flipped a thin plastic visor down from underneath the bill of his cap. Matterhorn reached up and flipped his own visor. Everything became brighter in a greenish sort of way.

"I added night vision visors to magnify ambient light," the Baron said.

"That helps a lot," Jewel said, relieved the passage was larger than it had felt in the stifling darkness. Still, she hated being underground.

"And here's something to make it easier for us to keep tabs on one another." The Baron handed out glowing yellow patches. "Put these reflectors on the heels of your shoes. There's a patch of the same material on the back of our caps. Seeing the water nymph behind Jewel he said, "Sorry, Sara, I only brought three caps."

"I can see fine. Besides, I don't produce any body heat."

"Will you be all right down here?" the Baron asked.

"It may be hard to stay with you if the air gets drier," she said.

"Maybe you should return to the vial. Then we'll be sure not to lose you."

"All right," Sara agreed, "if you promise to let me out as soon as you can. I don't want to miss anything."

"I promise."

Sara's jewelry clattered to the floor when she atomized into the vial.

Jewel adjusted her cap and tried to stop shivering. Matterhorn sympathized with her, having been a recent victim of his own phobia. Squeezing her shoulder he said, "Since you got to be first off the cliff, I'll go first in the cave."

With that, he led the trio forward and down. The blade of his Sword gave enough light to make the visors unnecessary. An eerie stillness replaced the clamor of the falls as they moved under the plateau they had jumped from a half-hour ago.

They had no way of knowing this would be a one-way trip.

Spelunker's Paradise

AARON the Baron was the only one with much spelunking experience. Running his hand along the tunnel's ebony sides he said, "Feel these walls. We're in a lava tube. Flowing lava can develop a shell of cooled magma. The molten rock keeps moving underneath and leaves behind a hollow tube."

"I've been in a lava tube before," Matterhorn said with a shiver. "The Ape Cave near Mount St. Helens. It's the second longest tube in the world." What he felt too embarrassed to add was that he had wandered away from his family and gotten hopelessly lost in the lower cave. It wasn't the first time his curiosity had led him into danger, but it was the scariest. When his flashlight died of exhaustion, the darkness was so thick and terrible that he had to close his eyes for a more manageable shade of black. He might still be down there if not for a kind elderly couple with a lantern who showed him the way out.

"Knowing how this cave was formed won't tell us where it goes," the Baron said. "We'll have to discover that for ourselves."

"Elementary my dear Watson," Matterhorn said in a poor British accent. "All we have to do is keep going straight." He pointed with his Sword, thankful its light wasn't dependent on batteries. But going straight was only possible for five more minutes. Then the passage split in two.

"Now which way?" Jewel wondered out loud.

Matterhorn held up his index finger and replied, "As Yogi Berra once said, 'When you come to a fork in the road, take it.'"

The Baron rolled his eyes. "Sherlock Holmes, Yogi Berra. Who's next, Yoda?" He turned to Jewel and asked, "Anything in the legends about this?"

She shook her head.

He took a small LED light from his pocket and shone its laser-like beam down one branch of the tunnel, then the other. In both cases the light seemed to go on forever. "Any ideas?"

"I picked the wrong way on the river," Jewel said. "You choose."

"Since you picked wrong," the Baron said, "I'll pick right." He produced a piece of chalk and drew a large arrow on the wall pointing back to the entrance. "This will help us find our way out. Remember the first rule of spelunking."

"Which is?" Matterhorn asked.

"Never go into a cave," Jewel said with an uneasy laugh.

"Exit takes more effort than entry," the Baron corrected. "Good spelunkers always plan with their return in mind."

"I've a mind to return to the surface right now," Jewel said. "You can come get me when you find the Sasquatch."

"We need to stay together," the Baron said. "Don't worry, we won't let anything happen to you." He glanced at Matterhorn who nodded his assurance before leading the way into what he hoped was the longest leg of this stone wishbone.

After a few hundred yards, Matterhorn questioned their choice as a foul breeze wafted by. He grimaced and pinched his nose shut with his fingers. "What's that smell?"

"I don't know," Jewel said, sniffing the rancid air. "I've smelled it since we started this way. And it's getting stronger. Don't tell me you're just noticing it?"

"Of course not," Matterhorn fibbed to protect his ego. A sizzling jolt reminded him why the Talis he carried was called the Sword of Truth. He yelped and dropped it like a hot poker. He tucked his smarting hand into his armpit and did the pain dance.

The Baron's laughter filled the tunnel.

Jewel clicked her tongue at the Baron and asked Matterhorn if he was okay.

"I'm just a slow learner," Matterhorn mumbled as he rubbed his sore palm. The Sword remained lit so he had no trouble finding it. He gingerly picked it up with his left hand and started forward again.

"I didn't notice the smell before," he said to Jewel, "but I'm picking it up now. If it becomes any more obnoxious I say we go back and take the other tunnel. This might be the way to the latrine."

The Baron and Matterhorn adjusted to the catacomb-like atmosphere around them while Jewel grew more agitated. At least the passage was roomy as far as caves go. Jagged lava stalactites stabbed down into the passage, but none far enough to furrow their bobbing brows. Stubby stalagmites jabbed up from the floor in odd places, making an obstacle course of the cave.

The one bright spot for Jewel was the strange iridescence now surrounding her. It was as if the passage had been sprayed with liquid moonlight. "Matterhorn, could you turn off your Sword?" she asked.

Matterhorn obliged. When their eyes adjusted to the dim light of their headlamps, the walls came alive with multicolored glitter.

"It's so pretty," Jewel whispered. She reached toward the luminescence. "What is it?"

The Baron grabbed her arm. "This beautiful stuff goes by an ugly name. It's called cave slime. It's a form of light reflecting bacteria. If you touch it, you'll kill it."

"I don't want to do that," she said, retracting her hand.

"I've been to some remote places," the Baron said, "and I'm always amazed at how the Maker decorates His creation. Even the parts no one sees."

The Travelers admired the view and enjoyed a snack of energy bars and water before pressing on. Matterhorn noticed that the shinier the walls got, the more slanted the floor became. No more forks or side passages came along to confuse them. They kept up a good pace for the next twenty minutes. Still, a growing unease crept over them as they burrowed downward like blind earthworms. This unease bloomed into full panic when the cave began jumping up, down, and sideways.

Another quake! This one was more powerful than anything they'd experienced topside. Being aboveground during an earthquake had been frightening. Being underground was absolutely terrifying!

The violent motion rolled the trekkers into a human cue ball that ricocheted down the tunnel, bouncing off stalagmites in a dangerous game of bumper pool. The jumble of arms and legs finally smacked into a solid wall and shattered into three dazed and bruised pieces.

Matterhorn felt the rocks, but not the pain, as he tumbled in the dark. He felt every twist and turn in surreal motion; an elbow jabbing into his left eye, his foot catching in someone's pack straps, the surround-sound of falling stones.

He lost the Sword almost immediately.

Then he lost consciousness.

Tunnel of Doom

THE sides of the hardened lava tube withstood the tremor. The roof did not collapse, but the floor was now tilted at a steep angle and dead-ended into a slab of stone.

"Whew!" the Baron grunted. He struggled to sit up. "Everyone okay?"

Jewel moaned. "You mean other than feeling like I fell down a flight of stairs?"

"On top of me most of the way," wheezed Matterhorn from between a rock and a hard place. He was still in shock from the fall; that's why he didn't notice the pain until he tried to push himself off the floor. The agony that screamed up his arm was different from the sting of the Sword. Even before he saw the awkward angle of his wrist he knew his arm was broken.

Matterhorn had a high pain threshold. He'd taken his share of hits in kendo. The bamboo *shinai* raised nasty welts, even through the protective body armor. Once, he broke his index finger in a soccer match while stopping a penalty kick. He refused to let the coach pull him and played the rest of the game without allowing a single goal.

He'd cracked a rib bodysurfing in the ocean.

He'd even been stabbed in the leg by a would-be killer.

But this pain was fiercer than all those injuries. Matterhorn rode the wave of nausea to the black edge of consciousness and hovered there.

Realizing something was wrong, Jewel crawled to Matterhorn's side. Her adept fingers soon found the problem in the dim glow of her headlight. "His arm is broken," she told the Baron as she helped Matterhorn sit up.

The Baron began scrounging in his pack for his first-aid kit. He had lost his cap in the tumble and had to feel his way to the square plastic box. Inside he found the pain pills left over from when he'd fractured his collarbone. Stumbling over to the two haloed figures, he said to Matterhorn, "Take these." To Jewel he said under his breath, "We'll have to set the bones. At least it's not his sword arm."

"What do we do now?" she whispered back with a calmness she didn't feel. "I don't want to die down here."

"We've made it this far. The Maker will see us through."

The Big Shaker had broken more than Matterhorn's arm. It had also split the floor of the cavern behind the falls. Water gushed into the cave and down its slanted throat much faster than the Travelers had covered the distance. The first wave soon splashed into the stranded spelunkers.

"The quake must have sprung a leak in the pool!" the Baron shouted when the frigid water hit.

Jewel stared at the stone wall that blocked their path. "Can we make it back the way we came?"

Aaron helped Matterhorn to his feet and answered, "No way. The water's coming too fast."

"I don't suppose you brought any scuba gear," Matterhorn said.

The Baron's eyes brightened. "I've got something better." He reached in his pocket for Sara's vial.

"I can't be gone for a second without you getting into trouble," the water nymph said when she grasped the situation. She was glad to be able to save the day—again— by quickly creating an ice barrier to stop the flow.

This deliverance would last only as long as their air supply, Matterhorn realized. He slumped against the wall and slid to the floor. The water lapped at his chest. The pain in his arm throbbed with every heartbeat and he tried to slow the one to ease the other.

Jewel couldn't stop shaking. She rubbed her arms and asked Sara, "Is there any way you can get us out of here?"

"That will take some doing if the cave is flooded," she replied. "Do you want me to go check?"

"No!" the three humans shouted. They knew if the ice broke while Sara was gone they would be goners.

Sweeping the area with her headlamp, Jewel soon found the Baron's cap hooked on a stalagmite. A short distance away she located Matterhorn's Sword, hilt-deep in a pile of debris. She brought it to him and he increased its light with a thought.

The Travelers silently surveyed their stone tomb.

Matterhorn fought for clarity through the pain and the pills. He couldn't just sit here waiting for death. He leaned his head against the stone and stared upward. It dawned on him that this wall was different from the others, more ragged and edgy. He ran his fingers over the rough surface. There was no cave slime on it.

With difficulty he stood, turned and raised his Sword higher. The wall was only eight feet high and stopped well short of the roof. But that wasn't the amazing part. A broad brown face beamed down on him with a Cheshire cat grin.

"G'day mates. Need a lift?"

Break Point

THE Baron snapped his head upward at the sound of the Australian accent. He realized at once what had happened. The quake had caused this section of the passage to break and drop below the rest of the tunnel. The ledge above them was actually the cave floor; and there on its lip squatted Nate the Great.

"How did you get here?" the Baron burst out.

"Let's get you out of there," Nate said, extending a hand. "Then we'll talk. Wounded and sheilas first."

The Baron and Jewel managed to get Matterhorn partway up the wall. Nate grabbed Matterhorn's good arm and helped him the rest of the way. Next came the Princess, the packs, and the Baron, who hugged Nate like a long lost brother. The two men, however, could not have been more different.

Aaron's face was angular, stubble-chinned, and white. Nate's was round, brown, and fringed with wiry black hair. His sideburns and beard were the same length as the steel-wool hair on his head. Between his eyebrows and moustache was a flat nose with flared nostrils. His dark eyes seemed large, as did his ears, but only by Western standards.

Born in the bush of central Australia, Nate was large for an Aboriginal, standing just under six feet and weighing just over 180 pounds. He had a short neck, wide shoulders, long arms, deep chest, and thin legs compared to his upper body. His physique was apparent because he wore khaki shorts and a tank top. There was a kangaroo-skin bum bag resting in the small of his back and a dingo-hide belt around his waist from which dangled various pouches. A short boomerang carved from mulga wood nestled against his left hip. He had on a most unusual pair of sandals. They were pure gold with emerald-studded soles. The green gems sparkled against the black floor.

"Bonzer trick with the ice," Nate said to Sara as she floated up beside them. He obviously knew who and what she was.

"Thanks," she replied.

"This crew's kept you busy," Nate chuckled.

The Baron frowned. "How do you know that?"

"Been following you since the portal, mate. Easy as tracking a herd of turtles."

"Who are you?" Matterhorn asked. "How did you get down here?"

"There's an alcove ahead," Nate said. "Let's yak there."

In a few minutes the five were sitting around a lighted can of paraffin at a wide spot in the tunnel. Once settled, the Baron introduced Nate the Great and Matterhorn to one another. Jewel already knew the bushman. "What were you saying about following us from the portal?" the Baron asked.

"You and the dunny rats on your tail," Nate said.

"Dunny rats?" Matterhorn asked.

"Vermin. Two of them have been stepping on your shadows since you got here. I've been stepping on theirs." Nate inspected Matterhorn's arm as he spoke.

"I have a very good sense for people and animals," Jewel said. "I didn't detect them."

"The creatures look like Bigfoot but aren't."

"Careful!" Matterhorn cried.

"How do you know they aren't Sasquatch?" the Baron wanted to know.

"Disguises are good," Nate said, tickling Matterhorn's palm and tugging each finger. "Found a piece of fur where one scratched against a tree. It's genuine, but they're not."

"Have you seen Bigfoot before?" Jewel asked.

Nate nodded and rested his other hand just below Matterhorn's elbow.

"What's not right about these two?" she pressed.

"They don't stink," Nate said. Then, without warning he tightened his grip and yanked on Matterhorn's hand.

Matterhorn screamed in pain at this unexpected assault.

"Steady, mate," Nate soothed, not loosening his hold. "That break needed to be set. Best get it over with."

"You could've warned me!"

The bushman gave Matterhorn a toothy grin. "You would've tensed up like a tick on a dingo."

Jewel bent forward to study the arm. "He's right," she told Matterhorn. "The bones are back together. Now you can heal."

The Baron inflated the air splint from the first-aid kit and eased it onto Matterhorn's forearm. "This will keep the break immobile," he said.

Jewel found a yellow bandana in her pack and made a sling.

The stab of agony was gone, replaced by a pulsing, yet bearable, ache. What Nate had done might have been for the best, but Matterhorn determined to keep a close eye on this frizzy-haired wild man.

Returning to the conversation that had been so rudely interrupted, the Baron asked, "What did you mean when you said the Sasquatch don't stink?"

"Everything has its own scent," Nate explained as patiently as a tour guide instructing eager tourists. "I could've tracked your smell with my eyes closed."

The Baron sniffed his armpit. "We've been in the water so much we haven't had a chance to get ripe."

"Any creature with body heat gives off an aroma," Nate said. "Humans smell different from dogs, which smell different from wolves. Bigfoot have their own scent."

Jewel knew what Nate meant. Her sense of smell was more acute than Matterhorn's or the Baron's. "Is that what we've smelled in the cave?"

Nate nodded. "Wait till you get close to a Bigfoot. Bigstink's more like it. A mix between BO and methane. One Bigfoot puts out more gas than a herd of cattle."

"And the creatures following us don't smell right?" the Baron said.

"Don't smell at all," Nate replied.

"If they're not Bigfoot, what are they?"

"Wraiths in disguise," Matterhorn said with a flash of insight. "They must have followed the Queen."

Dark Spirits

Chapter 17

WRAITHS," Jewel said with a start. "That's what Queen Bea was afraid of."

The Baron nodded. "We ran into one on our last trip. Matterhorn killed it."

"The Sword killed it," Matterhorn corrected.

"What are wraiths?" Sara asked.

"This is as good a time as any for a background briefing," the Baron said. Having spent more time in First Realm, he knew more about the wraiths than the others. "There is a Hall of Portals where Queen Bea is from. The Hall is called the Propylon and those who serve there are known as Praetorians. They are the elite Guardians of the portals used for time-space travel."

Sara, who had never been off-world before, nodded. To a creature like her, nothing seemed unbelievable.

"As with all moral beings," the Baron continued, "Praetorians have a choice to obey or disobey their calling. In the long history of First Realm, a few have chosen to use their high position for selfish and evil purposes. When these renegades are discovered, they are stripped of their powers and exiled. They become wraiths of their former selves, but are still very formidable. They hate the Maker and all who serve Him. They have sided with those who killed Queen Bea's father."

Sara wanted to know more, but Jewel whispered, "I'll tell you what happened later."

"Praetorians don't time-travel, except for their captain," the Baron said. "It's too risky. But wraiths seem willing to take the chance in coming to Earth."

"How come the one in Ireland looked human," Matterhorn asked, "while the two Nate has been tracking look like Sasquatch?"

"Apparently they can take any form they want when they travel. That will make them as hard to find as they are to kill."

Matterhorn shivered as he recalled his battle with the wraith. Now two more such creatures were hunting them. If Nate had managed to find the Travelers, so could these dark spirits.

But wait a minute. How *had* the bushman gotten here?

"Followed you to the edge of the plateau," Nate answered when asked. "Came down last night to have a lookabout."

"Where's your parachute?" Matterhorn wondered.

"Don't have one."

"Then how'd you manage?"

"Trade secret."

The Baron brought the discussion back to the present. "Any signs of the Sasquatch-wraiths down here yet?"

"No. Checked both arms of the Y you passed. They lead to the same place."

"Where's that?"

"A hollow volcano that puked its guts out eons ago. That's where the Bigfoot live. Wouldn't call it a city, though. More like a couple of villages." Turning to Sara, he said, "You blocked the water in this tunnel, but there's nothing keeping it out of the other branch. The flooding will cause problems for the Bigfoot."

"Are the villages in danger?" Jewel asked in alarm.

"For certain. Unless there's an outlet on the other side of the mountain."

"And if there isn't?"

Nate patted his neck. "The Bigfoot better grow gills in a hurry."

Matterhorn lumbered to his feet and stretched. His joints were stiffening and he wanted to get moving before he seized up altogether. Besides his broken arm, his right ankle was slightly sprained and he could feel a garden of colorful bruises blossoming on his backside. He noticed the Baron rubbing his left knee. Only Jewel seemed none the worse for their tumble. "Since we don't have gills ourselves," he said, "we'd better find the Band of Justice before this mountain becomes an indoor swimming pool."

"You have the light," Aaron said. "You have the lead."

Sara excused herself to go back and strengthen the ice wall she had hastily made.

Matterhorn limped into the unknown with Jewel glued to his side. The Baron fell in step next to Nate. "I haven't had a chance to thank you for bringing the mountain mint to camp yesterday. It really helped."

"You're not welcome."

"Why not?"

"Didn't bring it."

"Then who did?"

Nate said nothing.

The Baron finally figured it out. "You mean it was the bogus Bigfoot? Why would they do that? They want to destroy us, not help us."

"They need you to find the Band of Justice," Nate pointed out. "You need to be alive to do that. They're smart enough to know real Bigfoot won't come within a hundred yards of them because—"

"I know," the Baron interrupted. "They don't stink right."

"They'll keep their distance until you get what you came for, then they'll take it from you."

"Do you know where they are?"

"No."

From the front of the strung-out group Matterhorn tried hard to listen backwards. He caught most of what was being said, including the part about not knowing where the wraiths were. He spoke over his shoulder to the Baron. "How do you think the dark spirits followed the Queen?"

"I have no clue."

The party lapsed into an eerie silence. They trekked deeper into the mountain, picking their way around quake debris. Several minutes later Matterhorn turned to do a head check. Jewel's hat glowed a few yards in front of the Baron's, followed by—darkness.

Nate the Great had disappeared!

Green Giants

MATTERHORN stopped and sucked in a breath to shout for Nate, but the Baron put a finger to his lips. "No sense warning the Sasquatch we're coming. Don't worry about Nate. He knows what he's doing."

"Did anybody hear him slip away?" Jewel quizzed. "Where could he have gone?"

Not far, it turned out.

A hundred yards back, Nate had scurried up the wall and wedged himself between two stalactites. Pulling his legs up, he covered his shirt and shorts with dark shinskin. He pointed his toes down and lowered his forehead to his knees so that his black hair faced forward instead of the whites of his eyes, which reflected light. He blended into the dark and became invisible in the span of four heartbeats.

For him that meant six seconds.

Nate was great at disappearing when he wanted to. He preferred to work from the shadows. That Sword gave off too much light; it hampered his night vision. The others made too much noise. And in this closed space their scents clogged his ability to smell danger.

When the others started forward again, Matterhorn said to the Baron, "That guy must be part ninja."

"The ninjas were assassins," the Baron said. "They used darkness as a cloak for evil. Nate serves the light."

"Now that you mention light," Jewel interjected, "is that what I see ahead?" She drew their attention to a faint oval down the passageway. Matterhorn retracted his blade so they could see better. They slunk through the widening tunnel and soon arrived at the hollow heart of the prehistoric volcano.

An immense cavern opened before them, suffused with soft light from ragged skylights punched into the steepled roof hundreds of feet above. The sunshine nourished a wild variety of plants, shrubs, and stunted trees that covered the floor and crowded partway up the insides of the mountain.

"It's like an indoor forest," Matterhorn gasped.

"It's divine," Jewel said as somewhere in the distance a choir of birds warmed up for the evening service. She noticed pools of rainwater collected in natural stone basins under the skylights. "Sara will love this place."

In the middle of the chamber, beneath open sky, a small lake filled the throat of the once fire-breathing beast. The Baron pointed up and said, "Those holes were steam vents at one time. The giant one in the center was the main blowhole. And look at all the stuff growing in here. Plenty of sunshine and water, cooled lava to insulate the walls. It's like a giant nursery!"

"If this is a giant nursery," Jewel said with a gesture, "then those must be the giant gardeners."

A group of tall creatures stood by a stream that poured from a second tunnel a hundred yards away and gushed toward the lake.

"A bunch of Bigfoot," Matterhorn said. "And we're the first humans to see them." The manlike beasts were similar to the mental picture he had of the Sasquatch— except for one contrary detail. He checked to make sure his night-vision visor was up. "Is it the light in here," he said, "or are those things *green*?"

"They look green to me," Aaron said.

The thick hair on the Bigfoot reminded Matterhorn of pine needles. It carpeted everything but their palms and faces, which were wide and ape-like. The Bigfoot had sloped brows, flattened noses, and fleshy jowls. Their large eyes glowed red with reflected light, showing them to be nocturnal creatures. Below the neck they were barrel-chested and slump-shouldered. Their arms seemed too long for their bodies, their legs too short. The biggest creature stood over eight feet tall, the shortest was around seven feet. The smaller ones were obviously female. The group was bristling with gestures and grunts. They seemed to be arguing about the water now pouring into their private lake.

"That tunnel must be where the other branch of the cave comes out," Matterhorn said. "We won't be going back through the waterfall entrance. I hope there's another exit."

Bigfoot have big ears and one of the females heard the newcomers talking. She spotted the humans and squealed.

Voices froze in mid-grunt.

Heads turned like turrets.

Red-laser eyes locked on targets.

Not sure what to do, Matterhorn waved a greeting with his good arm. "Yell-O!"

One of the larger males bent and picked up a rock. He rolled it in his long fingers until his grip was just so then wound up like a softball pitcher and hurled it at the intruders with blinding speed.

Matterhorn had drawn his Sword and stepped forward when the Bigfoot had picked up the stone. The Queen had charged him to protect Jewel, and that's what he would do.

The fastball was on target.

But so was the Sword.

Quicker than the eye could follow, it deflected the rock with a shock that knocked Matterhorn off his feet. "Yeow!" he bellowed as he landed on his already bruised backside.

The pitcher snarled and picked up a larger stone. Other Bigfoot also reached for rocks. Before they could unleash their deadly volley, the tallest Sasquatch barked a restraining command. A moment later he started toward the humans. The other Bigfoot watched him go but did not drop their rocks.

Blocking out the pain, Matterhorn stood and flowed into *tai*—correct fighting stance—learned from hours of kendo training: shoulders squared with hips, right foot in front of left, weight slightly forward. His sword grip was firm, yet relaxed. In the normal, two-handed grip, the left hand provided the power while the right gave guidance. Matterhorn had only his right hand now; the Sword would have to provide its own power.

The Baron drew his switchwhip and extended the poison-tipped lash.

"Don't do anything stupid," Jewel warned.

"What!" Matterhorn barked. "Like trying to save our lives!"

"The Sasquatch is more curious than hostile," Jewel said. "Let him make the first move."

"Even if it's ripping my head off?"

"Ssshhh."

The Bigfoot planted himself ten feet away from the Travelers but his scent kept coming. It was the smell from the cave, only stronger. Nate was right. These creatures stank!

Seymour and the Band

T HE Baron walked up next to Matterhorn and blinked his watering eyes. The smell reminded him of a feedlot he had visited with his grandpa. The stench coated the top of his mouth and the back of his throat. He put away his weapon and pulled a small metal box from his pocket. He took out a plastic plug and stuck it in his right ear. Then he put a round, clear patch on his Adam's apple.

"What's that?" Matterhorn asked out of the side of his mouth.

"A self-programming universal translator. Let's see how long it takes to pick up Sasquatch." Facing the towering creature, the Baron raised both palms to show he was unarmed. "My name is Aaron the Baron. What's yours?"

Silence.

"All I hear is English," Matterhorn said.

"The Bigfoot has to say something before the translator can learn the lingo." He spoke to the Sasquatch again. "We mean you no harm. We come in peace."

Raised eyebrows but no response.

"Say something, big guy."

The Sasquatch scratched his ribs and stared at these stubby, hairless wonders with their dull eyes. His expression brimmed with curiosity. Or was it contempt?

While the men played with their toys, Jewel used her animal telepathy to read the Bigfoot as she'd read the bear a few days ago. Both creatures radiated raw power, yet this one was much more intelligent. Focusing on the expansive face three feet above her own, Jewel saw supreme confidence. He knew he could easily kill these strangers if it came to that. Above his luminous, wide-spaced eyes she caught a glint of red. Studying it, she saw patches of dirty white peeking through the tangled bangs on either side. She stepped closer to Matterhorn and said, "Check out his forehead."

Matterhorn had been staring at what gave the Bigfoot their name. The creature's foot was fifteen inches long and eight inches wide, with five long toes. At Jewel's suggestion, Matterhorn raised his sights to the colorful bump. "Biggest pimple I've ever seen."

"Try ruby," Jewel said, "as in the Band of Justice. He's wearing the Talis. And from the looks of the band, he's had it on for quite a while."

"Do you suppose he knows what it is?" Matterhorn asked.

"One way to find out." And before he could stop her, she walked within arm's length of the Bigfoot.

"Hold it," the Baron said, grabbing Matterhorn's shirt. "Let her try."

Jewel reached out and took hold of a massive, hairy hand. She stroked the palm for almost a minute. Then she placed it on the left side of her head. Holding it there with her left hand she used her right hand to put the creature's other hand on the right side of her head. There was hardly room for all of his fingers. He could have squished her skull like a grape.

The Bigfoot and Jewel stood that way for a long time, his hands on her head, her hands on his. All Matterhorn and the Baron could do was wait.

Near the end of their silent dialogue, the Bigfoot squatted so that his eyes were level with Jewel's. She rubbed his cheeks and touched his forehead above the ruby. At last he stood and returned to the other Sasquatch, who were as anxious to learn what had happened as Matterhorn and the Baron were to question Jewel.

"What did you find out?" the Baron asked.

Jewel didn't answer right away. When she did speak, it was in a respectful tone. "He's amazing, very sensitive and bright. He's chief of the Bigfoot. They call him "One Who Sees Farther" or "Sees More" for short."

"Seymour the Sasquatch," Matterhorn said with a smile. "How were you able to communicate? The Queen didn't say anything about the Band working both ways."

"We understood each other," Jewel said. "Maybe the Band amplified my natural empathy. However it happened I could see the pictures in his mind." She sat down and rubbed the tension from around her eyes. The Baron flopped beside her and handed over a water bottle.

After a noisy drink, Jewel continued. "He's curious about us, who we are, where we come from, what we're doing here. He's also concerned about our weapons. He has to decide if we pose a threat to his tribe."

"Threat," the Baron said. "Next to them we're children. But then, he's never seen humans before, so he doesn't know what to expect."

"That's not completely true," Jewel said. "His ancestors have had contact with a creature like us."

"How can that be?" Matterhorn said. "This area is supposed to be uninhabited."

"The Sasquatch have an old song about a man who brought them the Thinking Stone. That's what they call the Talis. The chief of the Sasquatch wears it so he can understand the others. Seymour has worn it for many seasons. I think it's increased his IQ. The song is beautiful. It tells how the Giver came long ago to the Salmon Waters. He made friends with the tribe and put the Band on the head of the strongest Sasquatch. The Giver made them understand that it was a sacred treasure, something to cherish and protect."

"Did he tell the Sasquatch it also had special powers?" the Baron asked.

"They're very smart," Jewel said, "much smarter than apes or gorillas. They soon learned how to use the Band to communicate. It's one of the reasons they've built such a strong tribal structure."

"Then they're not likely to part with it," Matterhorn observed.

Jewel nodded. "Probably not. However, the song says the Giver would return someday for the Band. That may be why Seymour stopped the others from killing us; because we look like the Giver."

"The Giver must have been the Praetorian captain," the Baron said. "But he's dead now. Do you suppose we can convince Seymour that the Giver sent us for the treasure?"

"I wouldn't try," Jewel said with a stern glare, "because it isn't true. We *can* say the original owners sent us to retrieve the Band. I'm not sure Seymour will accept that, though. And right now he has more pressing business." She looked at the water pouring from the other cave. "Seymour knows the earthquake caused this flooding. He was puzzled why we came out of this tunnel instead of more water. I told him about Sara and the ice wall she built. He wants her to make a wall in the other tunnel. I said we would ask her to do it when she returns. This would go a long way in winning his trust."

Thinking aloud, the Baron said, "In the meantime we should check for another outlet from this place."

"I asked Seymour about that," Jewel said. "There's a tunnel at the far end of the cavern. He hopes it can handle the water flooding in from this side. Sasquatch don't like water. That's one reason they live underground. It rains too much outside."

"That may be why they stink," Matterhorn said.

"Has Seymour sent someone to make sure the other tunnel wasn't damaged by the quake?" the Baron asked.

"It's not that easy," Jewel sighed. "That side belongs to the Browns."

"The Browns? Who are they?"

Wave Pool

PRINCESS Jewel leaned against the wall near the cave they had come through a short time ago. It had been a long and grueling day. Her side hurt and her psyche was taut with the stress of being underground. The mental contact with Seymour had also been draining. He was an intimidating presence, almost human in intelligence, yet beastly wild.

Matterhorn touched her shoulder in concern. "How are you holding up?"

"Just tired, that's all."

"Who are the Browns?" the Baron asked again.

"It seems there are two tribes of Sasquatch living in here," Jewel replied, "and they are enemies. Seymour tried to explain it to me. The Greens—Seymour's clan— came to America long ago across an ice bridge."

"Must have been the Bering Strait between Alaska and Siberia," the Baron put in. "It froze during the various ice ages and connected the continents."

"Anyway," Jewel said, "the Sasquatch moved south until they came to the Salmon Waters. My guess is the Columbia River. They love fish, and so they stopped there. Over time they adapted to the pine forests and their thick hair evolved from brown to grayish green."

"You said Bigfoot don't like water," Matterhorn interrupted. "So how do they fish?"

"They love the taste of salmon more than they hate getting wet. When Seymour thought about fishing, I got an image of a Sasquatch standing in the shallows and swatting salmon out of the stream. The others catch the fish like footballs. It's a game to them. When they have enough, the wet Sasquatch rolls in dirt and pine needles to get dry. It's pretty funny."

"I'm sure it is," the Baron said. "But get back to the Browns."

"In the not too distant past, another bunch of Bigfoot crossed the ice and came down the coast. Sasquatch view time differently, so I can't tell how long ago that was. Anyway, the newcomers haven't been here long enough for their coats to change. They're still brown. The Greens resent the Browns since they compete for food and living space. And when the Browns found their own way into this underground paradise, the Greens attacked them. The fighting was fierce, but the tribes were evenly matched. Neither could drive out the other. Today they live in a tense stalemate—the Greens on one side, the Browns on the other."

Closing her eyes, Jewel faltered. "I've seen the battles in Seymour's mind. They hurl rocks at each other and use clubs or bare hands. They are incredibly strong. Seymour doesn't like the fighting, yet he has to protect his tribe. The chief before him was killed by the Browns. Seymour knows the fighting has to stop someday, but he has a lot of bitterness over the—"

Just then Nate came barreling out of the cave behind them. "Make like lightning and bolt!" he yelled over his shoulder. "NOW!"

Matterhorn, the Baron, and Jewel stumbled into Nate's wake as he sped past. His tone left no room for arguing. They followed him at a dead run toward the lake.

The Sasquatch near the other tunnel stared in wonder at the sudden flight.

When Nate reached the water he stopped to help Matterhorn, who could not swim with a broken arm. The Baron inflated the airbag on Matterhorn's pack and then his own. Nate pulled Matterhorn toward the center of the lake while the Baron and Jewel put an arm each through his pack straps and paddled behind.

The quake began as a slow rumble deep in the earth. It shook the cavern floor and then climbed the walls to rattle the roof. Chunks of rock fell and burst like bombs. The shrapnel wounded several Sasquatch as they scurried about in terror. There was no place to hide.

Meanwhile the humans bobbed like rubber toys in a bathtub. The lake was deep and narrow, which made the waves sharp and choppy. The frigid water numbed Matterhorn's broken arm, along with the rest of his body. Without the airbag he would have drowned. So would the Baron and Jewel, who clung to the pack between them. "Didn't we almost drown together already?" the Baron joked through chattering teeth.

Nate coped by rolling into the fetal position. He filled his lungs with great gulps of air that kept him afloat like a beach ball. He had led the others here because it was the safest place to ride out the quake since it put them beneath the open crater.

The seismic shocks lasted over a minute, which seemed like forever to the humans and Bigfoot trapped inside the mountain. When the violence subsided and the lake settled down, the exhausted foursome floundered to shore.

Jewel sat on the stony floor, arms wrapped around her legs to control her shivering. "How did you know the q-quake was c-c-coming?" she asked Nate.

"Felt it," he said, pointing to his feet. "Seismic waves travel through rock like waves through the ocean."

"This must be the quake Queen Bea warned us about," Matterhorn said. He readjusted his soggy sling. The feeling was returning to his arm—the feeling of pain!

"This would register as a whopper on the Richter scale," the Baron said, "but it hasn't been invented yet."

Matterhorn had trouble hearing the Baron. He tilted his head sideways and tried to pound the water out of his ears. It took him several seconds to realize that the roaring wasn't in his head. It filled the chamber and bounced from wall to wall, crashing into its own echo. Looking back he saw water spouting from both tunnels now. It billowed outward then flattened into great satiny sheets. "Sara's ice wall must have shattered!" he yelled.

"Where is she anyway?" Jewel cried.

"No worries about Sara," Nate reassured them. "Water nymphs can take care of themselves. We'd best see to the Bigfoot."

Chapter 21

MORE light filtered into the chamber now because several of the roof vents had been enlarged by the quake. From the relative safety of the lakeside the Travelers saw that several Sasquatch had been hurt. Those still on their feet were dragging their companions away from the flooding. Both tunnels were now spewing water like broken fire hydrants. "Nate's right," Jewel said. "We've got to help them."

"I should've brought a bigger first-aid kit," the Baron muttered as they started toward the quake victims.

"I've got some medicines we can use," Jewel said, patting the pouches on her belt.

As they approached the disorganized Bigfoot, Matterhorn remembered the rock-throwing incident and thought about drawing his Sword. He decided against it, not wanting to give the wrong impression.

The Sasquatch were indeed suspicious, as if the humans had somehow triggered this disaster. A few reached for stones when the unwelcome strangers got close.

"We'd better find Seymour before we get killed," Matterhorn said nervously.

"That him?" Nate nodded toward a path through the shrubbery leading to a series of shallow cavities in the mountainside. Seymour was supporting a female whose foot had been crushed. Nate put his fingers to his mouth and gave a loud, piercing whistle. Every head turned at the sound, including Seymour's.

Jewel waved both hands in the air and cried, "We want to help!"

The chief looked at her blankly.

Thinking quickly, Jewel reached for Matterhorn's broken arm and pretended to set the bones.

Matterhorn winced in pain and said, "I hope he's good at charades."

Seymour understood the mime. He howled a safe-passage order and his tribe went back to collecting their wounded. When the humans caught up to the chief, he shifted his burden to another Bigfoot and conferred with Jewel as they had earlier, hands to head. After they finished, Seymour headed uphill with the humans in tow.

The Sasquatch village was honeycombed along the volcano's inner wall. There were no buildings or free-standing structures, just sleeping niches scraped out above an open area used for tribal gatherings. Now the place looked more like an emergency room. A dozen Sasquatch were laid out in various states of trauma with more on the way. Seymour checked the casualties with Jewel at his side.

After these initial rounds, Jewel reported that two Bigfoot had been killed and that some of the injured might not make it through the night. "I have some herbs and teas to prepare. Can you gather dry wood for a fire and boil some water?"

"Fire's risky," Nate said. "These creatures haven't seen it except for forest fires. Could cause a panic."

"Get the wood anyway," Jewel said without hesitation. "I'll explain it to Seymour."

"Is it safe to go off without his protection?" Aaron asked.

"He told the tribe to leave us alone—for now. But I wouldn't go too far in case you run into some Bigfoot who haven't heard the word."

This was a distinct possibility since there were dozens of Sasquatch bustling about.

A half hour later Jewel watched the boiling pot hanging over a crackling fire. It proved not to be a big deal. The Sasquatch knew about fire but didn't bother with it. Their fur kept them plenty warm and they couldn't imagine burning perfectly good fish.

As the sky darkened Jewel made the rounds with her teas and medicines. Some would not accept the steaming potions while others were desperate for anything to relieve the pain. Nate and the Baron showed the Sasquatch how to set broken bones. Gradually their assistance was accepted and appreciated. Matterhorn fussed with the fire and fumed at not being able to do more. He felt for the patients, having a painful injury of his own.

When they ran out of things to do, the tired Travelers sat around their fire and ate supper. Below them the flooding continued. The Baron massaged his sore knee and said, "This place will be an aquarium in a few days if this water doesn't have a way out. We've got to make sure the tunnel across the cavern is open. Jewel, can you persuade Seymour to take us into Brown territory tomorrow?"

"I can try," she said.

Matterhorn pointed to the patch on the Baron's throat and asked, "How did your translation gizmo do?"

"Pretty well. I should be able to speak with Seymour myself soon." He took the plug from his ear and held it in the light of his headlamp. "This earpiece analyzes voice patterns while the throat patch converts speech into modulated sound waves. The two units are wirelessly synched. When they've picked up enough vocabulary and syntax, they can translate what's heard into English and what's said into the corresponding language."

Matterhorn whistled softly. "Did you invent that?"

"No. U-Trans are standard issue for Travelers. They're preprogrammed with most languages, and what they don't know they can quickly learn. It's how Queen Bea can speak perfect English," he added. "Hadn't you ever wondered about that?"

Matterhorn hadn't.

The Baron put the device in its metal case and plugged it end to end into a second, identical case. Green lights blinked three times on both units. Then the Baron unplugged the boxes and threw one to Matterhorn. "Welcome to the club. Now your unit has all the data from mine." He repeated the process with the boxes handed to him by Nate and Jewel.

"Why didn't I get one of these?" Matterhorn asked as he put in the earpiece.

"For the same reason you didn't get any specialized training," the Baron said. "You're different from other Travelers. The Praetorians selected us; the Sword of Truth called you. Queen Bea told me it's never happened before."

"Makes you special," Nate said, touching his forehead in salute. The gesture was genuine, not mocking.

This attention embarrassed Matterhorn. "I may be special, but I'm not 'Great.' Where'd you pick up that tag?"

"From being such a large baby," Nate said. "Mum said having me was like birthing a watermelon. Always been big for an Anangu."

"How old are you?" Jewel asked.

"Fourteen." This made him the oldest of the group. He was also the most traveled, both in normal life and as a Traveler. "At the mission school," Nate continued, "the first books I read were about a boy detective named Nate the Great. That made the nickname stickier."

When he finished speaking, the bushman plucked a small hide pouch from his bum bag and put a pinch of what looked like salt mixed with green flecks in his mouth. He worked it around with his tongue and rinsed with water.

"Sand and peppermint," he responded to Matterhorn's puzzled gaze. "Works better than toothpaste." He offered the pouch and said, "Try some."

Enemy Territory

NATE went exploring the next morning while the Baron and Matterhorn took Jewel to find Seymour. The chief was easy to locate and soon he and Jewel had picked up where their last discussion had left off. Standing nearby was the Bigfoot who had thrown the rock yesterday. He was recognizable by the brownish fur on his chin that made for an off-color beard.

Wanting to get some data for his U-Tran, the Baron said, "That's quite a throwing arm you have." His voice sounded garbled to Matterhorn, but the noise seemed to make sense to the Sasquatch.

The creature walked over and stared down at the strangers who had come just before the shaking. Did their arrival anger Mother Earth, or was she upset that the tribe had not properly welcomed them?

Handing a rock to the hairy creature, the Baron said, "Show me how you get that kind of speed."

The Sasquatch palmed the stone, then dropped it at Aaron's feet.

Matterhorn tensed for trouble, but the creature just stooped and selected a larger rock. He wound up and zinged a pitch against the wall near the sleeping niches.

"Strrr-ike!" the Baron cried.

The Sasquatch jumped back and picked up another stone.

"It's okay," the Baron reassured the skittish creature. He slowly picked up a rock with his left hand and mimicked the Sasquatch's underhanded throw. "Like that?"

The Sasquatch threw again with three times the speed of the Baron's toss. They traded throws for a few minutes, then the Baron said, "Now try it overhand." He selected a baseball-size rock and pegged a perfect strike of his own. Back home he was an All-Star Little League pitcher with a couple of no-hitters to his credit.

The Bigfoot responded to the challenge, trying to copy the strange motion. His first attempt barely missed Seymour's head, which earned him a sharp rebuke.

Jewel scowled at the Baron. "Can't you play somewhere else?" She turned back to Seymour, who was waving his arms and shaking his massive head in disagreement.

"Come on, Thrower," the Baron said to his new friend. "We need more room."

Matterhorn walked over to listen to Jewel and Seymour. "Too . . . dangerous," he heard Seymour's gravelly voice croaking in his right ear. This thing works, Matterhorn thought, tapping the earpiece.

"We have to try," came Jewel's velvety response. "The water is rising."

Seymour glanced at the expanding sea and his shoulders sagged. "Well," he said at last. He gestured for several Sasquatch to join them.

Jewel shook her head. "Not a good idea," she said. "We won't get safe passage. The Browns may think you are attacking."

Seymour made a growling noise deep in his chest that the U-Tran couldn't translate.

"We don't want to put you in danger," Jewel said. "Send someone to guide us across. That's all we're asking."

This made Seymour indignant. He rose to his full height and Matterhorn thought the Bigfoot was going to backhand Jewel halfway into next week. But she stood her ground and repeated her request.

"Someone's got to check the other tunnel," Matterhorn said. "Just point me in the right direction."

Seymour scowled at Matterhorn and thundered, "I am the One Who Sees More. I fear no Brown!"

"Certainly not," Jewel replied. "But the last thing you need now is a fight. They may let us pass if they don't feel threatened."

"They . . . not understand," Seymour said. "Your speech . . . poor." He tapped the ruby on his forehead to indicate that it was the only reason he could understand the strangers. "The Browns will kill you."

"The flooding will do that if we don't do something," Matterhorn spoke up. Patting the hilt on his hip he added, "We can take care of ourselves."

Looking down into Matterhorn's eyes the chief saw courage. "I take you," he said finally.

"Good," Jewel said. "Let's go."

Seymour led them downhill and along a curving path at the base of the mountain wall. Several Bigfoot followed at a distance. This made Jewel nervous until Seymour snapped at them to go back.

The yelling attracted the Baron and Thrower, who were not far away. Thrower refused to stay behind and Seymour didn't object.

It took thirty minutes for the party of five to cross beneath the crater and into Brown territory. The central lake was fast becoming an inland sea. Fallen pieces of roof stuck above its expanding surface like coral reefs. Circles of sunlight floated on the tide that flowed from the ruptured tunnels.

Dark shapes began to appear on either side of the group. They were being surrounded by rock-armed Bigfoot. To Matterhorn these Browns looked like the Greens—same muscular builds, same intelligent faces and reflective eyes, which now scanned the trespassers.

The Browns recognized Seymour as the Green chief by the icon on his brow. But what were these strange creatures with him? Only curiosity made them hold their fire.

Matterhorn drew his Sword and its light scared the Sasquatch back several yards.

Seymour halted and snarled an "away" at Matterhorn. Then he addressed the Browns. Sasquatch communication seemed to be mostly gestures tied together with occasional growls. The gist of Seymour's speech was a demand to be taken to his Brown counterpart. His tone and bearing were fearlessly regal. Regardless of color, he was a chief and expected to be obeyed.

For their part, the Browns considered him with contempt. One of them pointed at the humans and demanded to know what they were. Seymour refused to say anything about the "strangers from outside," except to their chief.

The Browns argued among themselves until the leader of the patrol smacked the loudest protester up the side of the head—end of discussion. The intruders would be taken to the village. They could be killed later if necessary, something the leader made clear with a graphic gesture.

"Ouch," Matterhorn said to the Baron. "I hope it doesn't come to that."

The Browns tightened into a hairy cocoon around their prisoners and started walking. Along the way they attracted more company so that by the time they reached their clearing the fur ball had grown to more than thirty Bigfoot. Their smell was so rank that Matterhorn couldn't keep from gagging.

Jewel took a mountain mint leaf from a pouch and shredded it. She put the flakes in her nostrils and offered some to Matterhorn and the Baron, who did likewise.

Mercifully, the end of the cocoon twisted open and the patrol leader nodded toward a group huddled around a young Sasquatch. Gooey red blood oozed from an ugly cut above the youth's right ear and matted the rusty fur on his limp shoulder. The female who cradled the lad in her lap glanced up at the visitors. She panned from Seymour's headband down to his tiny entourage.

Touching the Thinking Stone, Seymour said, "I am One Who Sees More."

"I know you," the female growled in a deep bell voice. "What are these?"

"Strangers from outside . . . came with the waters."

Matterhorn cringed at being linked to the flooding. What if the Bigfoot decided the humans were the cause of the crisis?

Sure enough, the Brown's next question was, "Did they bring this trouble?"

Seymour looked from Jewel to Matterhorn to the Baron and shook his head. "They are like the Giver," he said. "They come to help."

Without waiting for more of an introduction, Jewel slid around Seymour and knelt in front of the female. This uninvited move brought a swift reaction from the Browns.

Good Medicine

SEVERAL Sasquatch surged toward Jewel, but the seated female restrained them with a raised hand. Jewel ignored the danger, being absorbed in the shared pain of this mother and child. The lad had lost a lot of blood since being felled by a chunk of ceiling. His eyelids drooped. Saliva dribbled from the corner of his mouth. His wound was too broad to scab over properly. A few more hours and he would bleed out.

Jewel began chanting in Chinook, asking the Maker for wisdom about what to do. Her soothing voice was the only sound in the clearing for a long time. She massaged the child's head while she sang. Slowly she brightened with an idea. Reaching into a belt pouch, she produced a palm full of fine white powder. She showed it to the mother before dusting it on the gaping wound. Next she took three long, porous leaves from a different bag, wetted them from her water bottle and applied them as a dressing.

The crystals swelled in the warm fluid to form a gossamer crust and seal the wound. Jewel put shavings of willow bark in her remaining water and gave it to her patient to drink, after which she sang him to sleep. When she finished, she stood and patted the mother's shoulder.

"Will he live?" the Baron asked softly.

"If he hasn't lost too much blood," Jewel said. "At least his skull's not broken."

The Sasquatch rose with her son in her arms. She was seven feet tall and almost as broad as Seymour. She said something that was followed by the sound of falling rocks. The Sasquatch were disarming.

"The chief has extended her hospitality," Jewel confirmed. "We are not to be harmed."

"The chief's a female?" Matterhorn said in surprise.

"Don't look so shocked," Jewel said. "Many tribal groups are matriarchal. They submit to the rule of their better halves."

Matterhorn ignored the dig since it had been delivered with a smile. "What happens next?"

"A powwow," Jewel said.

Seymour and Thrower sat down and motioned the humans to join them. The Brown chief carried her son to one of the wall niches, which looked similar to the sleeping grooves in the Green village. When she returned and sat opposite Seymour, Jewel got up and went to her side. This move pleased the chief. She called two males to complete the circle before motioning for Seymour to speak.

Matterhorn didn't need the U-Tran as Seymour acted out his tale. The wobbling back and forth indicated the earthquake. Hands jabbed skyward, then thwacked on the ground, illustrating the deadly reign of stones. Arms swooshing forward meant water spurting from the tunnels.

None of this was new to the Browns, but they listened respectfully to the Green chief because he wore the Thinking Stone. They knew of its legendary power.

Pointing eastward, Seymour asked about the tunnel beyond. Was it open?

The chief looked to the male on her left. He shook his head and pancaked his hands together to show that the cave had collapsed.

Bad news, Matterhorn thought. He had a good mind for math and spatial dimensions and did some quick calculating. With the drain plugged, this chamber would fill quickly. And long before the water reached the top, the air breathers inside would all drown. He leaned over and said to the Baron, "Unless we can stop the water somehow, we've only got a few days."

"Too bad the trees in here are stunted," Aaron replied, "or we could build rafts and float out the top."

"Noah and the Bigfoot," Matterhorn mumbled. "We'll need a better plan than that."

The Sasquatch had no idea how to cope with the flooding and the meeting ended with Seymour saying he would come back tomorrow for more talks.

Jewel and the Brown chief continued a private conversation after the circle broke up.

The Baron tried to talk to the Brown who had given the report on the tunnel, but all the Bigfoot did was repeat his pancake routine.

One curious Brown touched Matterhorn's yellow sling. Another yanked his ponytail. A third hooked a long fingernail into his belt, painfully scratching his waist. Matterhorn twisted away from the unwanted attention, feeling like an animal in a petting zoo.

Thrower came over and slapped the hairy hand away. The Brown snarled and turned on Thrower, but Seymour pushed Thrower toward the path.

Dim shafts of evening light slanted eastward across the water as they headed back to Green land. The expanding sea was lapping at the path by now and they had to watch their footing.

"Did you see the hatred on all those Brown faces when they first saw Seymour and Thrower?" the Baron said to Jewel. "Your healing touch with the chief's son saved their lives and ours."

"See it," Jewel shuddered, "I felt it. Seymour did a brave thing in approaching the Browns. So did Bertha in receiving us. It's the first contact between the tribes that hasn't ended in bloodshed."

"Bertha?" Matterhorn and the Baron said in unison.

"My name for the Brown chief," Jewel responded. "She's known to her tribe as 'Honored Birth Mother' because she's had several healthy offspring. Birth Mother, Bertha."

Matterhorn chuckled. "Seymour Sasquatch and Bertha Bigfoot."

"It's not funny," Jewel said. "This could be the beginning of a peace process."

"It'll be a short process if we don't find a way out this volcano," the Baron said.

Matterhorn had a terrible thought. Maybe the reason there's no solid evidence of Sasquatch in modern times is that they never made it out.

Color Line

Chapter 24

NATE was waiting for the others by a fresh camp-fire.

"Where have you been all day?" the Baron asked, taking off his boots and warming his feet by the fire.

"Around," the bushman replied. He was cutting the ends off thick yellowish pods with an unusual knife. The five-inch blade was black with red streaks and looked like a narrow stone arrowhead. The handle was carved from a wild boar tusk. "How'd the parley go?" he asked.

Jewel filled him in on the meeting with the Browns, including the part about the far-side tunnel being collapsed.

Nate nodded as if he already knew this. He split a husk with his thumb and ejected a string of olive-sized seeds and said, "I'm hungry as an anteater with a broken nose."

"What are those?" Matterhorn asked.

"Supper."

Jewel knew a lot about forest plants but didn't recognize these waxy beans. Perhaps because they grew underground.

119

"How do you know they're not poisonous?" the Baron quizzed. He didn't like trying new foods.

"Lift your shirt," Nate said.

The Baron looked at Jewel for an opinion.

"Black and blue I know," she said with a shrug, "and red and white. But yellow?"

The Baron reluctantly raised his shirt.

Nate squished a large seed and smeared the paste near Aaron's armpit. "Underarm skin's sensitive," he explained. "Toxins will cause a rash. If the plant doesn't harm the outside, it shouldn't hurt the inside."

"Clever," the Baron said as he pulled his shirt down. "But why not test it on yourself?"

"Easier to see a rash on white skin."

"Is that true?" Jewel asked.

Nate winked and went back to shucking pods.

Matterhorn laughed, thankful he hadn't been selected as the food tester. "While we're waiting for the word on dinner, let's review our situation, starting with the negatives. First, we can't get out the way we came in. Second, the exit tunnel is blocked so the water can't get out either. Third, our favorite water nymph isn't here to help."

"I'm worried about Sara," Jewel said.

"We all are," Matterhorn agreed. "For now we have to plan without her. On with the bad news: Fourth, we can't even raft out the top. There isn't enough lumber in here to get all the Bigfoot afloat. There must be a couple hundred Sasquatch between the Greens and Browns."

"Right direction," Nate said, "wrong number."

The Baron frowned. "What's that supposed to mean?"

"Don't have to get everyone out. Just me and you."

"What do you have in mind?" the Baron asked.

"Popping outside tomorrow and shutting off the water," Nate said as calmly as if suggesting a morning jog.

The Baron gazed at the roof arching overhead into darkness. "And just how are we going to manage that?"

"Climb out the nearest vent hole and hike to the falls," Nate replied. "As for stopping the water, I see you still wear your belly pack. Is it stocked like on our last trip?"

Nate was referring to the slim body-pouch the Baron wore under his shirt. Among other things it held a flat strip of C-4 plastic explosives. The detonators rested in the heel of his right boot. These were only part of the Baron's arsenal. His belt had five hidden tools while his pockets and pack bulged with everything from Chinese throwing stars to solar-powered electric eyes.

Their last trip had been to the Mayan empire in Central America. A mudslide had buried the entrance to a portal and a month of sun had baked the earth to concrete. The Baron had resorted to C-4 to blast open the tunnel.

Aaron patted his midsection. "Are you thinking what I'm thinking?"

"Blowing the mouth of the cave shut should tuck the stream back into its own bed," Nate said.

Matterhorn craned his neck backward. The nearest star-pocked vent hole loomed hundreds of feet overhead.

"How much rope you got?" the bushman wanted to know.

"Two rolls of 100-foot, 5mm Kevlar rope," the Baron said. He pulled a neon yellow coil from his pack and a second from Matterhorn's gear. They weighed one pound each. "I've also got a few metal spikes."

"You carry more stuff than an army surplus store," Matterhorn said. "Parachutes, climbing gear, night vision visors. Where do you get the money to buy all this gear?"

"There's a bank account Travelers can access with a special credit card," the Baron said. "I buy the equipment I need off the Internet and store it at my workshop in the Propylon."

"Where does the money come from?"

"Former Travelers mostly."

"*Former* Travelers?"

The Baron smiled. "Time travel is hard on the body. People can't do it forever."

"So what happens to them?" Matterhorn asked.

"They go on with their lives," the Baron said. "Get married, raise families, find careers, whatever." The Baron scrounged through his pack while he spoke. "They still stay involved with First Realm, looking for new recruits when needed, investing in the Traveler's Fund."

"What should Matterhorn and I do while you're gone tomorrow?" Jewel asked.

"Get the Bigfoot to work together on clearing the exit tunnel," Nate said.

"Not likely," Matterhorn snorted. "The Browns would have killed Seymour and us if Jewel hadn't saved the day. I can't see the two tribes cooperating."

"They're not that different," Jewel said, "except for their fur coats."

"There's more genetic variation within races than between them," Nate pointed out. "Still, color's a big divider. Jewel's people were herded onto reservations because of it. In my country, black babies were taken from their parents to be raised by 'civilized' whites."

Jewel nodded. Even though humans were more advanced than Sasquatch, they hadn't learned to be color-blind. From South Africa to North America people were persecuted for simply being a few shades different from their neighbors. "Perhaps the threat of extinction will be enough to get them to work together."

"I hope so," the Baron said. "But save the Sasquatch or not, we have to remember why we're here."

"To get the Band of Justice," Matterhorn said.

"What are you saying?" Jewel asked.

"If all else fails," the Baron replied, "we'll have to snatch the Band from Seymour and take it to the Queen."

"Can't you use the Traveler's Cube to take the Sasquatch outside?" Matterhorn asked.

"No. The Cube can only be used by Travelers. That's a cardinal rule."

"Why?"

"Because well-meaning Travelers would use it to save lives and avert disasters."

"What's wrong with that?"

"It would change history, and that's one thing First Realm will absolutely not allow."

Jewel and Nate nodded in confirmation of the Baron's words.

"If the Praetorians found out I'd done such a thing," Aaron continued, "no matter how noble the reason, the Talis would be revoked and our traveling careers would be over."

It was quiet for a long time after this. Finally, the Baron checked his side. Not finding a rash, they roasted the yellow seeds. The fleshy vegetable reminded Matterhorn of artichoke hearts.

"These taste like candle wax," the Baron complained.

Nate produced some dried mountain pepper leaves, ground them between his fingers and sprinkled the Baron's food. After one large bite, Aaron's nose began watering and the tips of his ears turned red. Sweat beaded on the back of his neck. The tiny flecks felt like acid on his tongue. The heat radiated upward and cleaned out his sinuses. "Aahhgg!" he cried, groping desperately for his water bottle.

Matterhorn's interest perked up at this reaction and he asked for a dose of the spice. To his more experienced taste buds, the pepper rated somewhere between serrano and cayenne. Not as potent as insanity sauce, but intense enough to make his own head sweat—just the way he liked it. "Have you ever heard of Scoville units?" he asked Nate.

The bushman shook his head.

"It's the heat index used to rate the capsaicin level in peppers," Matterhorn said. "Bell peppers have zero. Habaneros, the hottest peppers on earth, can pack more than 350,000 Scoville units. That's hot enough to melt the enamel off your teeth."

"Why not just swig gasoline and set your tongue on fire?" the Baron said.

Matterhorn rolled his eyes and reached for another pod.

Blown Assignment

T HE campers were awakened by a faraway shout. Nate's small face—haloed by light blue sky—shone down from above. A yellow strand of Kevlar rope reached partway down the inside of the volcano from the vent hole where he perched. The route up the inner wall to the rope went from steep to vertical and beyond.

"How in the world . . . ," Matterhorn began.

The Baron knew it had to do with Nate's Sandals, but he didn't take time to explain. Instead he got up and started stuffing items into his pockets, including a pair of gloves and some energy bars. He donned his red corduroy cap and clipped a water bottle to his belt. "Take care of my gear," he told Matterhorn as he headed out.

Scooting upslope to where the mountain wall steepened, the Baron considered how far he would have to free-climb to reach the rope, dangling what seemed like miles overhead. He chided himself for not bringing another coil, but when he'd left home his pack weighed over sixty pounds. At least he didn't have to heft it up this rock face.

Through the skillful use of cracks and bumps, he made it to the end of the line in a stressful half hour. From here the rope was anchored to pitons driven into fissures every twenty feet. It took the Baron another ten minutes to hand-over-hand climb his way to the vent. His arms ached, his neck and shoulders screamed, but it felt good to be outside.

Nate squatted on his haunches and watched Aaron crawl like an ant out of its hill. "You climb like a girl," he said.

"Don't let Jewel hear you say that," the Baron rasped. "She'll zip up here and challenge you to a duel. Besides, you cheated. Let's trade shoes and see who's faster."

"No time, mate. This volcanic slag will get slicker'n elephant snot on bamboo if it rains."

"You mean *when* it rains," the Baron said. "This is the Pacific Northwest."

The rocky slope was tricky and took all their concentration to navigate. But when they made it to more gentle terrain, they fell into easy conversation. From their previous trip together, the Baron knew that Nate had been a Traveler since he was ten years old. While on a spiritual quest to Uluru, a stranger had appeared to him who turned out to be a Praetorian. He explained about First Realm and traveling and showed Nate a special cave that housed a portal.

Curious about what Nate did when he wasn't traveling, the Baron asked him.

"Always traveling," Nate replied.

"Even when you're not portal hopping?"

Nate nodded. "Aboriginals don't build cities. We move with the seasons."

"What about school?"

"Half my year's spent in the outback, half at a mission school. My family taught me to read nature; the missionaries taught me to read books."

The Baron stooped to pick up a branch for a walking stick and got a good look at Nate's Sandals. "When did you get those?"

"A few months back."

Nate didn't offer any more information and the Baron didn't press.

When they stopped for lunch by a friendly stream, Nate went fishing. Instead of using a line and hook, he found a supple branch and tied one end to the other to form a loop. He draped his tank top over this to make a net and quickly bagged two large trout.

"That's not very sporting," the Baron said.

"Aboriginals are into survival, not sport."

The Baron built a fire and roasted the fish. Nate made stone tea by filling his animal-bladder canteen and adding a mixture of leaves and herbs. Using his shirt as a hot pad, he picked flat stones from the coals, dropped them into the bladder and let it simmer.

"Ummm, this is good," the Baron pronounced after his first sip. "You might say this drink really rocks."

"Please, don't," Nate groaned.

Walking away from the spot a few minutes later, Nate paused and looked back. "See anything?" he asked.

The Baron scrutinized the area and shook his head. They had left no ashes, no whiff of smoke, no rock out of place. Nate had seen to that.

"Leaving nature undisturbed shows respect for creation," the bushman said. "It also gives an enemy no path to walk."

They reached the base of the waterfall by mid afternoon. The pool was shallower than when the Baron had last seen it. That's because the river water was now pouring into the hidden alcove and down the tunnel.

From a vantage point off to one side, they peered through the mist at the rock formation behind the thundering waters. "Can you set a charge to drop that overhang to block the tunnel?" Nate yelled above the din.

The Baron pointed his stick at the ledge and shouted, "Can't tell! We'll have to find a natural crack to exploit! Ready to get wet?"

They made their way around the falls and into the alcove. The Baron climbed on Nate's shoulders and scanned the ceiling. He spotted a crevice running across the roof about five feet from the entrance. Something closer to the edge would be better, but this would have to do.

The Baron rolled his C-4 into a snake and stuck a wireless detonator in one end. He stuffed it into the crack, then he and Nate moved back outside. From a fair distance away he said, "If this works, that slab of rock should drop straight down."

"Use enough explosives?"

The Baron shrugged. "That's all I have." With that, he touched the stud on his belt.

The blast could barely be heard over the noise of the waterfall. The rock overhang shuddered, then creaked downward, as if hinged to the side of the mountain. A moment later the huge slab broke free and jabbed edge-first into the cavern floor. It toppled forward into the pool instead of backward into the alcove.

"Oops," the Baron moaned.

There was a loud crack as more chunks peeled like dead skin off the granite face and splashed into the water. Rather than blocking the tunnel, the rocks now deflected even more water down into the bowels of the mountain.

Nate slapped the Baron on the back. "Aim's a bit off, mate. Best get back and get our friends out."

The uphill climb and an afternoon downpour slowed their return trip. It was well after dark by the time they reached the vent hole and slid down the rope like spiders on silk. The Baron went first. He secured himself at the end of the line while Nate undid the rope from the top and free-climbed to his partner. They repeated this leapfrogging descent all the way to the cavern floor.

Last night's campsite was submerged.

Matterhorn and Jewel were gone.

Ambush

EARLIER that morning, after Nate and the Baron had gone to shut off the water, Matterhorn and Jewel planned their day over a breakfast of seeds. The chamber floor below them was flooding faster than expected. Broad bushes and stunted trees downhill from the Green village poked through the glassy surface like tropical islands.

"At this rate," Matterhorn said, "we won't be able to reach the Browns after today without swimming."

"And that's something the Sasquatch aren't good at," Jewel said. "Me either for that matter."

"Did you know what you were getting into when you agreed to become a Traveler?" Matterhorn asked.

"Not really," Jewel said, stirring her tea. "How could I? How could any of us? Traveling didn't used to be this risky. We watched and reported and didn't interfere. But since the trouble in First Realm we've become Talis hunters with dark spirits shadowing us."

At the mention of wraiths, Matterhorn felt the old wound in his thigh begin to throb. He rubbed his broken arm above the air splint and experienced a flashback of his tumble down the tunnel. "Traveling is definitely hazardous to one's health," he said. "You could have told the Queen you didn't want to come."

Jewel stiffened at this. "Just because it's gotten hazardous doesn't mean I want out."

"I didn't—"

"Everyone has a destiny," Jewel said over the top of his protest, "something we're meant to discover and do. When I was given the chance to Travel, to do what most people can't even imagine, I felt so blessed. So *chosen*. And if I checked out during the hard parts, I would be cheating my calling." She softened her tone when she realized she was preaching to the choir. Matterhorn had obviously made his own decision to obey his calling, a calling more direct and dangerous than that of other Travelers.

"I didn't mean to raise my voice," she apologized.

"That's okay," Matterhorn said. "I know what you're feeling. I was almost killed on my first trip but I was glad when I got the summons here. I swore an oath to carry the Sword and serve the Maker. What is it they say at weddings? 'For better or for worse, in sickness and in health, till death do us part.' "

Jewel laughed. "I trust it won't come to that."

"I believe we are protected until our work is done," Matterhorn went on. "I was scared spitless when I jumped off the falls, but I didn't die. And I don't expect to croak in this volcano." He patted the quote book in his hip pocket and added, "Davy Crockett once said, 'If a fella's born to be hung, he'll never be drowned.'"

Having finished breakfast, they put on their U-Trans—the units were fully functional now—and went to find Seymour. He was busy with a group of Bigfoot, the village elders Matterhorn guessed. Jewel went over and stood next to the seated chief. She rested her hand on his arm and thus tuned in to the discussion. It was twenty minutes before Seymour called a halt and stood up. He looked tired as he walked past Matterhorn and started across the cavern.

"Seymour's exhausted," Jewel said, falling in step with Matterhorn. "He and most of the Greens spent last night trying to dam up the tunnels. It didn't work. The current's too swift. He thinks if the Browns help they might be able to do it. That's what he wants to talk to Bertha about."

"It's too late," Matterhorn said, glancing over his shoulder. "The tunnels are almost underwater by now."

"You have a better plan?"

"Yes. But it involves Sara and I don't know where she is."

The path to the Brown village was knee-deep in water that made for slow going. Near the Brown village they were met by a patrol as they had been yesterday. This one was not so obliging. Two hulking Browns blocked the way and refused to move despite Seymour's insistence.

Jewel's animal sense went to red alert. "These aren't the same Sasquatch as before," she told Matterhorn as three Browns circled around to close the trap. "We're in trouble."

Matterhorn turned and drew his Sword one-handed. The light within the diamond blade gleamed as he faced the towering trio.

"If you kill them, we'll never get the Browns to trust us," Jewel said.

Before Matterhorn could reply, Seymour collared the closest Brown and flung him downhill into deeper water. Another Bigfoot bear-hugged Seymour from behind and jerked him off the ground. The Browns in the back moved to join the action, expecting to sweep the puny humans out of their way like toddlers.

Matterhorn had a different idea. It was called *shikake waza*, the kendo attack technique where a fighter strikes first. Heating his blade at the speed of thought, he swept it broadside on the Bigfoot like rattling a hot poker along a picket fence. He landed several scorching blows while darting beneath their wildly swinging arms.

The startled Sasquatch howled in pain and retreated. They beat at their smoldering fur and splashed water on their burns.

Matterhorn spun to help Seymour, but the chief didn't need any. He had flipped his attacker over his head and somersaulted onto the poor creature's chest. The blow cracked a few ribs and ended the ambush.

Or so it seemed until Bertha and a second squad of Browns appeared on the path ahead.

Vital Link

SEYMOUR began fishing in the water at his feet for rocks to hurl when Jewel ran past him toward the Browns. She sensed that Bertha had not come to finish them off but to rescue them. The Brown chief had not ordered the attack and was even angrier than Seymour that her tribe had broken the promise of safety she had given yesterday. Bertha had the bushwhackers hauled away and personally escorted Seymour's party toward the tribal circle.

"It seems some Browns don't want anything to do with us," Matterhorn said, pausing to wash the burnt hair off his blade and to dry it on his pant leg. Now that the fight was over his hands were shaking, even the one in the sling.

"You're pretty good with that," Jewel said.

"I've been practicing," Matterhorn said. "What now?"

"The two chiefs have to talk."

Matterhorn frowned. "We can't waste another day gabbing. Time is getting shorter with the rising tide. Can you think of any way to speed things up?"

Jewel laced her fingers together and cracked them in a series of pops. "Now that you mention it, I can." They had reached the village and Jewel grabbed Seymour's massive hand. She led him to where Bertha was just sitting down in her usual place. Nudging a scowling male aside, Jewel positioned the two chiefs together. Then she plopped between them and rested her hairless arms on their shaggy knees. In effect she was forming an empathic link allowing both Bigfoot to benefit from the Talis on Seymour's head. Instead of words and gestures they could now share thoughts and feelings and come to a meeting of the minds much sooner.

The sensation was overwhelming for all three participants. Matterhorn could only wonder at what was happening behind those wide eyes and taut brows.

Chaos is what was happening. Images strobed through the shared minds in panoramic 3-D. Neural pathways overloaded as sensations crashed into each other like bumper cars gone berserk. Nerve endings throughout their bodies tingled in what amounted to virtual reality.

Jewel pulled herself together and began asking questions to focus the mental trialogue. Would the tribes put aside their differences during this crisis?

Both Bigfoot were skeptical, yet knew they needed each other's help.

Could they work together to stop the flooding?

Not all Browns or Greens could be trusted in close quarters with their enemies. Some would seek revenge for past wrongs. The chiefs would have to handpick the work crews.

Would it be easier to stop the flooding or unblock the escape tunnel?

The water was so high in the Green tunnels by now that their only option might be to clear the Brown tunnel.

Were there any other ways out of the mountain?

A fleeting picture in Bertha's mind caused her to jump up and break connection with Jewel and Seymour. She stomped off, leaving a broken circle of bewildered Bigfoot.

Jewel understood what had upset the Brown chief. The image that Bertha did not want anyone to see was of a long, low passage snaking through porous rock. One end of the tunnel was concealed in a sprawling thicket on the backside of the mountain; the other end lay somewhere east of the Brown village.

This tunnel was how the Browns had first found their way inside. Its location was their most closely guarded secret. It was their emergency escape route if the Greens ever became strong enough to destroy them.

Jewel had managed to pick up an even more vital piece of information before Bertha broke away. Her tribe had decided to use this tunnel to sneak out of the volcano—and leave the Greens to drown! With their enemies dead, the Browns would have the whole territory to themselves.

Seymour had seen only a portion of a murky image before Bertha had disconnected. Not enough to place the tunnel or to pick up the Brown evacuation plan. He stood and rubbed at the headache behind his eyes.

Jewel got up and went after Bertha. "Don't let Seymour leave," she told Matterhorn.

"Where are you going?" he yelled after her, but she didn't answer.

Jewel found Bertha behind a boulder near the sleeping niches. She squatted with her forearms on her knees and surveyed the sea that would soon engulf her village. The relentless waters would drive them from paradise. She did not move when the human came up and put those soft, tiny hands on her shoulders. She had nothing to fear from the Small Ones. This one called Jewel had saved her son's life. Jewel was a friend.

The unspoken bond between them gave Jewel something to work with. She knew that Bertha had no remorse about leaving the Greens to die. Survival of the fittest was the way of things. If Bertha helped the Greens escape, the fighting between the tribes would go on till one destroyed the other. Better to let the mountain swallow the Greens.

Jewel scooted around to face Bertha. When they were eye to eye, Jewel thought and said the word, "Mother."

Bertha smiled at the small, childlike tone of voice. She played with Jewel's braid and repeated the word. "Mother."

"Will you leave me to die with the Greens?"

Bertha shook her head emphatically. Of course she would not leave Jewel. Her plan was to send Seymour away with the promise of help while asking the Small One to stay. Tonight, under cover of darkness, they would sneak outside and seal the tunnel.

"Can my friends come, too?" Jewel asked, her eyes not leaving Bertha's.

Bertha paused a moment and then nodded. "Friends."

What Jewel did next changed the course of Sasquatch history.

Friendly Persuasion

JEWEL pulled on Bertha's arms like a child dragging a reluctant adult off the couch. "Come," Jewel said. "I have something important to show you."

The Brown let herself be led back to the meeting circle. Matterhorn was entertaining the Bigfoot with his harmonica. He even let Seymour try the mouth harp to keep the Green chief occupied until Jewel returned. Seymour's fat lips fluttered as he blew wet air through the instrument. It filled with thick saliva and sounded like a kazoo being played underwater.

"It's about time," Matterhorn said when Jewel and Bertha arrived.

Rather than put the two chiefs together again, Jewel dropped Bertha's hands and walked to Seymour. She wrapped both arms as far around his thick waist as she could. "Friend!" she said with passion. "Friend!"

Bertha shook her head. "No Greens!"

"Friend," Jewel said again, tightening her grip to make it clear that she wouldn't go without him.

Bertha's features clouded in anguish. She did not want her new friend to drown. She also did not want to betray her tribe. The instinct to protect her own was strong. But so was her gratitude. Confused, she turned her back on the group and sat down. She hugged her knees and rocked sideways like the pendulum of a grandfather clock.

In the long silence that followed, Matterhorn slipped up next to Jewel and asked under his breath, "What's this all about?"

The Princess let go of the Sasquatch and pointed to the edge of the clearing. Once away from the Bigfoot, she explained about the secret tunnel and her gamble to use the concept of friendship to save the Greens.

Matterhorn gave a low whistle. Jewel's quick thinking impressed him, but he didn't think her ultimatum would sway Bertha. "If Bertha doesn't volunteer to show us the tunnel," he said, "we'll have to use force."

"Don't be such a Neanderthal!" Jewel snapped. "Trying to grab something from someone only makes them hold it tighter. Better to ask in love and hope for love in return."

"And if it doesn't work?"

"That's the risk love takes."

"If the Browns leave the Greens, would you really stay with them?"

The question surprised Jewel. "Yes, wouldn't you?"

Matterhorn thought for a moment. "I suppose so. Queen Bea ordered me to retrieve the Band of Justice and to protect you. As long as you're both here, I'm not going anywhere." With that, he went down to the water to wash out his harmonica.

Jewel returned to Seymour, who was anxious to go home. She explained that Bertha was struggling with whether or not to cooperate with the Greens, and they had to give her time to decide. She did not tell him about the tunnel.

By the time Matterhorn got back, the clearing was empty except for Jewel and Bertha. Seymour had refused to wait. Bertha had sent the Browns away to prepare for their evening exodus.

Matterhorn sat with Jewel and wondered if she wasn't expecting too much from the Bigfoot. Could they look to the future instead of the past? Could they understand and respond to friendship that went deeper than color? He sighed as he recalled that humans hadn't done very well at it. Why hadn't the Maker made all His creatures color-blind? That would have saved a lot of grief.

Across the way, Bertha rocked back and forth and wrestled with her thoughts. From Jewel she had caught a glimmer of a future that could be different from the past: cooperation instead of killing. Her higher instincts were stirred and something akin to hope sprouted in her heart like spring grass. If nature could start over every year, why couldn't Sasquatch? She would offer to share the secret of the tunnel in exchange for Seymour's promise to stop the fighting.

When Bertha came over and smiled her decision, Jewel jumped up and hugged her, crying with happiness in the Bigfoot's fur. Bertha hugged back, careful not to squish the Princess. Then she held Jewel at arm's length and pronounced Seymour's name.

"She wants to see Seymour," Jewel told Matterhorn.

"Then let's take her," Matterhorn replied.

"You have to come alone," Jewel said to Bertha. "No bodyguards."

The Brown chief understood this. As they walked downhill she ordered away the males who came to argue or accompany her on such a dangerous journey. It was a sign of their respect that they obeyed and let her go.

At the low point of the eastward trip the water lapped at Bertha's knees, Matterhorn's waist, and Jewel's chest. It felt as cold as the melted snow that was its source. Matterhorn and Jewel were half frozen by the time they reached the Green village. Matterhorn went to check on their gear, which they had stowed in one of the empty sleeping niches. Jewel and Bertha waited for Seymour under the watchful gaze of wary sentries.

When the Green chief arrived, he extended his hospitality as Bertha had done the day before. He called a circle of counsel and waited to hear what she had to say. As before, Jewel sat between the two chiefs and established an empathic link. The experience wasn't as jarring the second time.

Bertha thought right to the point. She imagined the secret cave and the Sasquatch flowing upward through it to safety. In her vision, the refugees were both Brown and Green. She was offering Seymour a way to save his tribe. But she wanted something in return. She was taking a great risk, one that many in her tribe would not understand. They would think she had betrayed them. Some might even attack when she brought the Greens back with her, as she planned to do. She had to know that Seymour would work with her toward peace and that things would be different on the outside—no more fighting.

Jewel understood that Bertha was doing more than saving the Greens. She was gambling on a better future for all Bigfoot. Her ante in this high-stakes game of survival was her tribe's most prized possession. Was Seymour willing to match her bet? That's what Bertha wanted to know as she stared at him over the top of Jewel's head.

It was Seymour's turn to count the cost of peace. "Sees More" had been so named for a reason. Wearing the Thinking Stone had amplified his natural intelligence. He had grown in his ability to acquire knowledge and to understand what was best for his tribe. Here was a chance to end the bloodshed and start over with the Browns.

Bertha had made the first bold move toward peace. He would answer in kind.

Peace Offering

SEYMOUR slid around Jewel to face Bertha knee to knee. Then he did something he never thought he would do. Slowly he took off the Thinking Stone and placed it on her head, combing her bangs around the ruby. The Greens around the circle went ape over this amazing turn of events. They began yelling and thumping their chests. Some threw dust in the air and flailed their neighbors with windmill arms. The sacred artifact that made them the superior Sasquatch had just been given to their foes. The symbol of ultimate authority now rested on a Brown forehead.

Jewel and Matterhorn looked on in stunned silence. Seymour had matched Bertha's courageous act of leadership. Would the Greens understand he was trying to save them from certain death by submitting to her?

Bertha touched the smooth gem and her eyes lit up. All Bigfoot regardless of color knew about the Thinking Stone. Its powers had given the Greens a great advantage in their struggle against the more numerous Browns. She even knew the legend of the Giver and his solemn charge to safeguard the Stone until his return. Before today Seymour would have died defending what he had just freely given her. Looking into his stern face Bertha knew he would still protect the treasure with his life. She rubbed the smooth area on his forehead where the band had rested for so many years. "Thank you," she said. "Thank you."

"Stone for safety," Seymour said. "Fair trade." Then he rose and began shouting and motioning to the gathering throng of Greens. They were to collect the children and wounded and follow Bertha back to Brown territory. There she would show them a new way outside. Greens and Browns would leave together and live together once all were safe. The old hatreds would stay inside the mountain.

Seymour made it clear that Bertha would lead, pointing to the Thinking Stone. Anyone who did not want to follow her could stay here and drown. Anyone who came along but caused trouble would wish they had drowned by the time Seymour got done with them.

The Sasquatch that the Baron had named Thrower began loudly reinforcing Seymour's instructions. He broke up a small knot of grumblers by banging two heads together and kicking a third protester in the rump.

There would have been a stronger revolt against Seymour's actions if not for the floodwaters swirling nearby. Bigfoot didn't even like rain, so the prospect of drowning was unimaginably horrible. Cooperating with the Browns was the lesser of two evils.

"Seymour did a very wise thing," Jewel said as Matterhorn helped her up with his good arm. "This is a great day for all Bigfoot."

"But not so great for us," Matterhorn said.

"What do you mean?"

"It would have been hard enough to talk Seymour out of the Band of Justice. No way is Bertha going to hand over her new symbol of authority."

"Let's worry about that once we're outside," Jewel replied. "Right now we need to get to the Brown village before the water gets any higher." She had no way of knowing that the volume of river water pumping through the tunnels had doubled due to the Baron's failed blocking maneuver.

By the time the Greens started their pilgrimage east a half hour later; the path was six feet underwater in places. Children were hoisted to parental shoulders. Jewel accepted a ride from Seymour. Matterhorn perched on Thrower like an overgrown parrot on a pirate. The Bigfoot had no neck to straddle; his sloped shoulders started at the ear and angled down into muscular arms. Matterhorn had to loop his right arm around Thrower's head to hold on.

The coarse fur felt supple, yet scratchy, through Matterhorn's clothes. Thrower's breath was surprisingly fresh compared to his body odor. He was eating a yellow pod like those Nate had discovered yesterday and offered one to Matterhorn.

Without a free hand, Matterhorn could only shake his head.

Thrower understood and raised the snack to Matterhorn's mouth. He took a bite of the pod and chewed. The juice from the seeds was refreshing, but the husk was like chewing Styrofoam. When he eventually had to spit out the yellow cud, Thrower burst into laughter that almost pitched Matterhorn into the water.

"Careful big fella!" Matterhorn cried. He wished he had Jewel's empathic powers so he could tell what was going on inside Thrower's giant green noggin. But he didn't, so he adjusted the throat patch of his U-Tran and began talking. The Sasquatch cooperated with the learning exercise and the chatter continued for the rest of the trip.

When the Green parade reached Bertha's village the Browns were ready to rumble, rocks and clubs in hand. Bertha bellowed for quiet and got it. The Thinking Stone on her head and Seymour by her side made it evident that she wasn't a prisoner. Far from it, she was in charge. She told of the new alliance required by their shared danger. The Greens would be going with the Browns to the tunnel. They had agreed to abide by her authority; she expected her own tribe to do the same.

Matterhorn waited with the Greens while Jewel went with Bertha and the Browns to make final arrangements for the exodus. It didn't take long as they had been preparing to leave all day. Soon Bertha was back with her young son in her arms. He was awake and alert, but still too weak to walk. Before setting out, she appointed two large Browns to help Seymour and Thrower keep order.

Standing on a rock ledge by Thrower and watching the furry brown and green caterpillar crawl away, Matterhorn prayed that the uneasy truce would hold. The procession climbed as far as it could up the inside wall of the cavern where the vegetation was more sparse. Even here the cold water splashed to Matterhorn's thighs. Jewel put her belt around her neck.

The farther from the center of the cavern they traveled, the darker it got. Matterhorn and Jewel relied on their night visors to see. The Sasquatch were used to the darkness, but *not* to the water. The stink of fear added to their noxious odor. The only thing smellier than a dry Sasquatch was a soggy, scared one. Matterhorn's nose clogged with the moist, liquid stench and he begged Jewel for more mountain mint leaves.

The last traces of sunlight had disappeared by the time they reached the escape tunnel. It was hidden by a clump of tall, prickly shrubs that resembled holly, except the berries were white. Since the need for secrecy was past, Bertha had the bushes torn away to reveal what looked like a keyhole in a huge granite door.

The narrowness of the passage meant they would have to proceed single file. Bertha decided that a string of Browns would go first, followed by a group of Greens, then another bunch of Browns, and so on until everyone was outside. Jewel would go with Bertha in the lead. Matterhorn would join Seymour in the second group. Thrower and his Brown counterpart would bring up the rear.

While the Sasquatch were busy sorting themselves into the right pattern, two shapes glided through the black water toward them as quietly as crocodiles. Matterhorn caught the movement and drew his Sword.

Upward Exodus

T HE "crocodiles" surfaced as Nate and the Baron. "Got room for two more on this expedition?" the Baron said as he sloshed up to Matterhorn.

"I think we can squeeze you in," Matterhorn said, putting away his Sword. "Do you prefer the Green section or the Brown?"

Thrower greeted the Baron with a loud grunt and a clap on the shoulder that knocked him back into the water.

Matterhorn laughed and helped his partner up, "Were you able to stop the flooding?"

"Just the opposite," the Baron admitted. He explained how his strategy to block the tunnel had backfired. "The Green village is underwater," he added. "So is the path between villages."

"How did you find us, then?"

Nate tapped his nose.

"Even I could smell it," the Baron said.

"This tunnel go topside?" Nate asked.

Matterhorn scratched his stubbly cheek and nodded.

"It's the Brown's top secret passage." He pointed to where Jewel was changing the leafy dressing on Bertha's son. "The Princess arranged a peace plan that involved Bertha showing us the tunnel. Seymour sealed the deal by giving Bertha the Band of Justice."

"He did what!" the Baron cried.

"Gave away the Talis," Matterhorn repeated. "I'm not sure we can take it from her without starting another war, but that's not our most pressing concern. We've got a lot of big bodies to get through that small hole. I wonder why we haven't started yet."

The problem was with the wounded. Bertha didn't know how to get her son and the other infirm Bigfoot through the long passage. The Sasquatch would have to crawl, which meant they couldn't carry the injured in their arms. The ceiling was too low for the wounded to be hauled piggyback and Bertha refused to let them be dragged.

Some Greens wanted to abandon those who couldn't make it on their own and an argument broke out. Matterhorn, Nate, and the Baron shoved their way to Bertha and Jewel while Seymour made it quite clear no one would be left behind.

"That's what has them jumpier than a mob of joeys?" Nate said. "No worries." He waded into the gloom and returned with several large, leafy branches. He showed Jewel and the Baron how to knot these into litters and started Matterhorn and Thrower stripping bark to serve as straps before going after more lumber.

When there were enough litters and harnesses to go around, Bertha dropped on all fours and entered the tunnel. A Brown male pulling her son was next, followed by Jewel and a Brown female.

Seymour was leading the first group of Greens into the passage when the air above the Baron shimmered and solidified. Sara glared down at him and demanded, "Were you going to leave without me?"

"Sara! You're alive!"

"Last time I checked," she said, pinching her cheeks.

"Where have you been?"

"Under a rock."

"No, seriously," the Baron pressed. "Where have you been?"

"Seriously, under a rock," Sara said. "I was working on my ice wall when the big quake hit. A slab of ceiling fell and trapped me in a shallow recess in the floor." She patted the bill of his cap. "You would be about this size if you had been there."

"How'd you get out?" Matterhorn asked.

"A great surge of water hit the stone and shifted it just enough for me to escape."

Nate poked the Baron and said, "Seems your blast did some good after all."

"I rode the wave into the cavern," Sara went on. "This place is filling fast. You air breathers are in trouble."

"I'd ask you to go back and freeze the tunnels shut," the Baron said, "but it's not important now. We're on our way topside." He found Sara's vial and removed the stopper. "In you go."

Sara crossed her arms in protest. "I want to stay out and help."

The Baron remembered not being able to find her when Matterhorn was missing at the falls. He thought about the last few days when no one knew her whereabouts. He knew nothing about the tunnel he was about to crawl into. He shook his head. "It's too risky. I don't want to lose you again."

Sara pouted, then dissolved like a genie into her bottle.

There was a commotion at the mouth of the cave and the humans went to investigate. Thrower would not let any Sasquatch in until Matterhorn took his spot behind Seymour. Matterhorn apologized for the delay and ducked in. While the Bigfoot were forced to their knees in the corridor, Matterhorn could get by with a crouch. There were sections where he could almost stand. The floor was steeper than the entrance tunnel, which gave him hope that the way out would be shorter than the way in. The walls were rough and veined with minerals, so this wasn't a lava tube.

Time passed in a straight line. There were no twists, bends or forks to slow things up. It was as if the way had been bored by a giant drill. Matterhorn's night vision visor and headlamp helped him avoid jutting rocks. He didn't need to light up his Sword, but his mind was on the blade and his plan to take it home with him.

Soon they would be aboveground. Jewel could charm the Band of Justice from Bertha and their mission would be over. Perhaps Queen Bea would show up like she had in Ireland to collect the Talis. Or maybe they would take it to her in First Realm. Either way Matterhorn wanted to keep the Sword the way the Baron got to keep the Cube.

He had already made preparations for the Sword's arrival. When his Great Aunt had died earlier that year, she left $5,000 to each of her nieces and nephews. Matterhorn put most of his money in the bank for college, but he talked his parents into letting him use some to start a sword collection. So far he'd bought a samurai sword of fine Japanese steel, a replica of a cavalry officer's saber from the Old West, and an English broadsword. They hung on the wall above his bed and would provide a natural setting for the Sword of Truth. He figured having the Talis with him would make it easier to be called into service at a moment's notice.

Matterhorn got so engrossed in making up a history of the Sword to tell his parents that he didn't notice the glimmer of light ahead. He didn't see Bertha crawl out of the hole on the side of a hill—or hear the crunching sound when a large rock cracked her skull.

Ensnared

BERTHA'S unconscious bulk was dragged into the bushes before the Sasquatch pulling her son came into the moonlight. He gave an exultant yelp at seeing the starry sky overhead. A moment later he saw a different kind of star as a tree branch broke across his forehead.

Jewel heard both the yelp and the crack and knew something was wrong. She approached the opening and peered out at the ghostly landscape. While not being able to see beyond the surrounding shrubbery, she could make out the drag marks on the soft ground. She stuck her neck out a bit farther—and was yanked upward by her collar.

The green Sasquatch holding her was nine feet tall. He was one of the two stealth creatures that had been tracking the humans for the past week. His leathery face wrinkled into a snarl as he said, "About time." Using his arm like a crane he swung her away from the tunnel and dropped her beside the unmoving Bertha.

Before she could scramble to her feet a second Bigfoot shoved her face-first into the dirt and snaked a thick vine around her hands and feet. Her capture had taken less than ten seconds.

The Brown female who came out next was ready for trouble. She dodged the first blow and charged her attacker, head-butting him in the chest. He clapped his cupped hands on her ears with enough force to rupture her eardrums. She let out a terrible scream and passed out from the pain.

The score was five to nothing in favor of the visiting team, with only Jewel and Bertha's son still conscious. Seymour was next up. Being chief of a tribe of Sasquatch was not an honorary position. He was a shrewd fighter whose natural instincts had been sharpened by the Thinking Stone. He rocked back on his haunches and blasted out of the cave like an enraged bull. The heavy branch meant for his head hit the ground behind him. Seymour somersaulted to his feet and took off downhill. Not because he was afraid of his enemies, but because he wanted to draw them away from the others.

If they had been Sasquatch, they would have chased him.

They weren't.

They didn't.

Seymour had no idea what a wraith was, and the wraiths had no idea what a Sasquatch was until just before their trip through the portal. They had assumed their hairy disguises to track the Travelers, which they had done until the unpredictable humans had jumped off a cliff. By the time the Sasquatch-wraiths made it down to the base of the waterfall and discovered the secret tunnel, it was already flooding because of the quake. That might have been the end of it if not for the chance sighting of a Bigfoot foraging for food. They followed the unsuspecting Brown to this tunnel on the backside of the mountain and set their snare.

Instead of going after Seymour, the wraiths turned to the shaft of light glowing by the tunnel opening and the man who held it—the Sword of Truth and Matterhorn the Brave.

Matterhorn knew what was happening as soon as he stepped outside. So this is where the wraiths had been, waiting for the rabbits to leave the hutch. He yelled down the passage, "We've got company! Everyone's been caught except Seymour; he ran off!"

The thought of facing two wraiths made Matterhorn's liver quiver. But he willed his body to act on what his mind believed: the Sword would protect him. He couldn't swing it with much force one-handed, but he didn't have to. One touch would destroy the dark spirits.

They knew it, too, which is why they kept away from the glowing shaft. The taller of the two picked up Bertha's son and splayed his massive hand on the youth's head, ready to unscrew it like a lightbulb. "Stay where you are," he ordered Matterhorn.

Nate and the Baron squeezed past the Bigfoot ahead of them and came out on either side of Matterhorn.

Instinctively the three formed a triangle with their backs and moved forward cautiously.

Tightening his grip, the Sasquatch warned, "Stop, or I will twist his head off."

The Travelers froze, except for the Baron's wrist, which snapped a Chinese throwing star at the Bigfoot's face. The creature swatted the chrome blade away as though slapping a mosquito. "Save your toys," he said with disdain. "I will take your Talis, however." His large red eyes moved from the Baron to Nate to Matterhorn to the unconscious Bertha. "I came for one and will leave with four. That makes this stinking skin more than worth wearing."

"Don't count your Talis before they're snatched," Matterhorn said, raising his Sword.

Suddenly, a loud grunt erupted behind him and Matterhorn spun in time to see the second Sasquatch jerk a small log from beneath the edge of a huge round stone. The rock rolled along a gouge and came to rest over the mouth of the tunnel. With that, the final piece of the well-laid trap was in place.

"You have two options," said the first wraith in a voice loud enough to regain everyone's attention. "You can resist, in which case we will kill you and them." He nodded to the wounded Sasquatch. "We will also leave the tunnel blocked and all the Bigfoot will drown." He made a gurgling sound in his throat and put on a mocking frown. "Or, you can come with us to the portal."

The wraiths would have already tried to kill them, Matterhorn knew, except that they needed the humans to carry the Talis. Being dark spirits they couldn't touch the Maker's handiwork. "Can't handle the Talis, can you?" Matterhorn taunted. "Light and darkness don't mix. Truth and lies—"

A heart-stopping scream interrupted Matterhorn's smug speech as the wraith holding Bertha's son snapped the youth's arm in two.

Unnecessary Roughness

MATTERHORN had never wanted to hurt anyone before, but had he been a few feet closer, he would have cut the wraith's head off and used it for a soccer ball. He was too angry to speak and it was Nate who finally said, "Leave the Sasquatch alone. We'll go to the portal."

The second wraith untied Jewel and ordered her to take the Band of Justice off Bertha and put it in her pack. After doing so she joined the others as the first wraith said, "Each of you must swear on the Sword not to fight or flee. Your oath will bind you as servants of . . ." He couldn't say the Maker's name.

"Will you swear on the Sword to move the stone if we do?" the Baron asked.

The wraith scoffed at the obvious trick. "You are wasting time," he said above the wails of the injured youth in his arms.

"We can't let others suffer because of the Talis," Jewel said. She put her hand on the Sword. "I swear by the Maker that I will not fight or flee, but will go with you to the portal."

Nate and the Baron followed suit.

From his quote book Matterhorn recalled the advice of Napoleon, "The best way to keep one's word is not to give it." But he could see no other choice. "I swear by the Maker that I will not fight or flee," he repeated.

"Good," said the wraith. He dropped his hostage carelessly on the ground.

"And I also swear," Matterhorn continued in a steel-edged tone, "that if you do any more harm to the Bigfoot, or try to hurt us, I'll—"

The wraith's animal laughter rang through the trees. "Big words for one so small."

"It's not my size you have to worry about," Matterhorn said. "I've seen what this does to your kind." The blade in his hand flashed, then went dark.

Jewel rushed toward the young Sasquatch even as his mother groaned from the bushes. Matterhorn removed his air sling and gave it to Jewel, who applied it after aligning the broken bone.

"We do not have time for that," the wraith scowled.

"Go stuff yourself," Jewel snapped. She gave the youth some willow bark to chew on and helped Nate carry him to his mother's side. Shielding her actions from the wraiths with her body, she took the replica of the Band of Justice that Queen Bea had given her and placed it near Bertha. The copy didn't have the power of the real Talis, but it would help Bertha and Seymour make peace between their tribes.

"Enough," the Sasquatch said. "Let us go."

"Move the rock first," Matterhorn said, adjusting his aching arm in the yellow sling.

Indicating the crest of a nearby hill, the Sasquatch said, "When we are up there." He started toward the spot while the other wraith piled the victims of the ambush in front of the tunnel. The idea was that the freed Bigfoot would be more concerned with their injured than with chasing after the humans. The wraith then shouldered the boulder aside just enough to open a small gap. And when the first Green male tried to squeeze through, the wraith smashed the creature's knee sideways, breaking his leg and clogging the opening.

The wraith bounded up the hill more like a gazelle than the 1,200-pound gorilla he was. In no time the humans were being hurried through red cedars and ponderosa pines toward the sunrise. The lead Sasquatch set a grueling pace with his long strides. The Baron, who was behind him, had to dodge bristly branches as they swished violently in the Bigfoot's wake. Nate and Jewel jogged side by side. Matterhorn trailed them and the second Sasquatch used a switch to make sure he kept up.

Topping a gentle ridge they reached a sparsely forested area awash in flat yellow light. Matterhorn's flesh and spirit were flagging. His arm throbbed. His legs throbbed. His head throbbed. He knew they had done the right thing by surrendering in order to save the Bigfoot, but he hated giving the Talis to the Queen's enemies. There had to be something they could do short of breaking their oath.

Finally Matterhorn's sleep-deprived body gave out. He stumbled, lost his balance, and fell. The Baron circled back to his fallen partner and propped him against a fallen tree. "We've got to rest," he told the wraiths.

Either Sasquatch could have tossed Matterhorn over his shoulder like a blanket and never slowed down. But neither wanted to get close to the Sword. The lead wraith spat on Matterhorn in disgust. "What the royals see in humans I will never understand. Such a weak species."

"Ever hear of scorpions?" Nate asked, sliding between the Sasquatch and Matterhorn. "Small but lethal critters you don't want to cross."

This obvious challenge angered the wraith. "I do what I want!" he bellowed, then made a lightning jab at Nate's head.

The furry fist caught nothing but empty air. Nate dropped to the ground and rolled between the Bigfoot's legs and sprang up like a jack-in-the-box, lifting the brute off the ground and dumping him on his back. Nate had a rope around the creature's ankles before his head bounced the second time on the hard ground.

The other Sasquatch was also caught off guard by Nate's feat of strength. He knew what the flashing emeralds in the bushman's sandals meant, but he was determined to kill the human. Before he could gather himself to lunge at Nate, the Sword of Truth flashed in his face.

Matterhorn was on his feet and staring up into the fiery eyes of his worst fear. At that moment he experienced what in kendo is known as *take kurabe to iu koto*, "the comparison of height." This is when a warrior sizes up the situation to see if he has the spirit to become taller than his foe. A determined spirit is more important than physical size and Matterhorn was determined to protect Nate, even though it meant fighting a nine-foot wraith.

One slash and it would all be over, yet Matterhorn didn't strike because of his oath.

The wraith had no such reservations about killing Matterhorn and Nate. There would still be two humans left to carry the Talis. And while he had great respect for the Sword, he had none for the one-armed man who held it. He tore a large, gnarled branch from a nearby tree and swung at Matterhorn's head.

Every nerve in Matterhorn's body wanted to jump at once: sideways, backwards, anywhere away from the savage blow. Instead, he braced himself and swung his Sword to meet the branch. What had Queen Bea said back at the portal: "All things are possible to those who believe." He believed the Sword was more powerful than the wraith.

He was either right—or dead.

Self-Defense

THERE was a sharp *fsssst* when the branch hit the blade and just the briefest flash of laser brilliance as the wood vaporized. The momentum of the swing twisted the Bigfoot completely around. The palms of his hands steamed and swelled with instant heat blisters. His eyes shot sparks of molten hatred at Matterhorn.

Meanwhile, the grounded Sasquatch had come to his senses. He sat up and grabbed Nate around the waist. He lifted the bushman over his head, careful to keep away from the Sandals. Matterhorn heard Nate's grunt and spun with such precise control that his blade stopped an inch from the Bigfoot's throat.

Once again he kept himself from killing a wraith, even as he wondered why he should honor his word to a dark spirit with Nate's life at stake.

Because it was given to me, said a voice Matterhorn instantly recognized. He did not bother to glance about for the speaker but formed a clear thought in response to the divine presence: Now that you're here, you can take care of these awful wraiths.

What makes you think I just arrived?

If you'd seen what they did to the Sasquatch—Matterhorn brought to mind the sights and sounds of cracked skulls and broken arms—you could have prevented it.

I see all the evil that goes on in creation.

And you don't stop it?

For the time being, I limit it.

Limit it? How?

The Sword of Truth flashed and the voice vanished.

The Talis existed as tangible expressions of the Maker's character and power, Matterhorn realized. They were weapons that could defeat evil if wielded honorably. He held the blade motionless and ordered the wraith to release Nate. "We swore not to fight but we said nothing about defending ourselves. Try to harm any of us again and you're smoke."

The Bigfoot tossed Nate to one side. These humans were more trouble than expected. Best to get the Talis to the Realm as soon as possible. Then there would be time to make them pay for their insolence. He stood and snapped the rope from his ankles. Without a word, he walked back the way they had come to make sure they weren't being followed. That would give him time to cool down.

"You have ten minutes to rest, no more," the other wraith said. He licked his sore palms and backed himself against a tree to scratch.

Matterhorn slumped down beside a mossy rock, exhausted and exhilarated by what had just happened.

"Our fearless foe has fleas," the Baron said under his breath.

"I hope they give him the plague," Jewel said.

The Baron removed the lid from a water bottle and handed it to Matterhorn. "You may be onto something," he said. "If we provoke the wraiths into striking first, we can defend ourselves without breaking our word."

"Don't push that too far," Nate cautioned. "The wraiths only need one porter. Three of us are expendable."

"Not if I can help it," Matterhorn said with more confidence than he felt. He took a long drink then poured the rest of the water on his head.

"What happened back there?" Aaron asked. "I thought you were going to kill that wraith."

"I wanted to," Matterhorn muttered, so tired now that the words dribbled down his chin. He didn't have the strength to speak of what the voice had said.

"Try these." Nate offered Matterhorn some round brown berries from a worn leather bag. "Thanks for covering my back."

The berries were so bitter that Matterhorn spat them out.

Nate grinned. "Forgot how rough these taste." Handing over a few more he suggested sucking instead of chewing. He also gave berries to the Baron and Jewel.

"Coffee beans," the Baron guessed after a few minutes. "They've got quite a kick."

"They've been, er, chemically enhanced."

"How?"

"Don't ask."

"Is it a family secret?"

"Only if you're a weasel."

Jewel winked at the Baron. "Leave well enough alone."

But he kept pressing until Nate finally said, "They've been coated with enzymes from a Luwak."

"A what?"

"Luwak. Member of the weasel family."

"You mean . . ."

"We're not the first ones to eat these beans," Jewel said. "I told you not to ask."

Matterhorn thought about ejecting his second batch of berries but decided against it. He felt new energy stirring in his rubbery limbs and didn't care where it came from. He adjusted his sling and leaned toward the Baron. "Can you use your Cube to get us out of here? We're all Travelers so it won't violate the rules."

Aaron shook his head. "I could only transport two of us. It takes an incredible amount of energy to uncoil a dimension and hold it open long enough for matter to slide through. And the Cube needs time to recharge between uses."

"Okay," Jewel replied. "You and Matterhorn take the Talis to safety. That's all that matters."

"And leave you and Nate behind? No way."

"We can outrun these brutes," she said, fingering her onyx earring.

"You're the one who told us Bigfoot are faster than horses," the Baron reminded her. "And these are super Sasquatch."

"We swore we wouldn't run," Matterhorn said with an authority that ended the discussion. "We'll stand by our word and by each other." A moment later he added, "That is if someone will help me get up."

Forced March

THE Bigfoot that Nate had toppled returned from his walk and announced, "Time to go. I do not want to stay in this skin any longer."

Falling in line, the group set off. Matterhorn double-timed next to the Baron and quietly said, "The wraiths don't need their Bigfoot disguises now. Why not shed them?"

The Baron shrugged. "Maybe they can choose whatever form they want when traveling, but can't change back until they return to First Realm. Just like we can't revert to our natural ages."

"Is that where they're taking us?" Jewel asked. "First Realm?"

"Not to the Propylon," the Baron replied. "The Praetorians control that. There must be a portal in heretic hands somewhere."

"There are more things in heretic hands than you imagine," sneered the wraith behind them.

"Best keep our thoughts to ourselves," Nate advised the others.

For several foot-weary hours the wraiths drove them toward the portal cave like cattle to slaughter. Under different circumstances, Matterhorn would have enjoyed the scenery. Intense volcanic activity and ice age glaciers had shaped this rugged terrain. Rainbows of delicate wildflowers painted the basalt terraces along the hillsides and scented the brisk air. Ferns grew to prehistoric size. Lush moss draped trees of every shape and size.

All afternoon they hiked under the sharp-eyed gaze of mountain goats and big horn sheep. Overhead, bald eagles surfed the coastal winds between jagged peaks that wore snowcaps on their green heads. Since the escape tunnel came out on the backside of the volcano, the trek to the portal was much shorter than the Travelers' original route. This geographical fact, plus their unflagging speed, brought them within sight of their destination before dusk.

The wraiths showed no signs of fatigue but the humans were spent. It had been nearly two days since any of them had slept. The caffeine effect of the Luwak berries had worn off long ago.

The Baron's lungs hadn't fully recovered from his recent bout with pneumonia and Nate had been supporting him the last half hour. Matterhorn was almost too exhausted to care what happened anymore. A quote from his book kept running through his brain: "Being defeated is temporary; giving up is what makes it permanent." Still, he was ready to quit. Only a miracle could save them now.

Jewel and Nate weren't so gloomy. Both knew they were being tracked by real Bigfoot. Jewel sensed Seymour and others nearby. Nate had picked up telltale signs his captors had missed. Within sight of the portal he stopped and told the wraiths, "I need a bathroom break."

"Me, too," Jewel chimed in.

They weren't thinking about their bladders; they wanted to give their would-be rescuers a chance to act.

But the wraiths were too close to home to tolerate any more delays. "No!" barked the one in the lead. "I do not care if—"

The rock swooshed in hard and struck him in the right temple with a sickening crack. Blood and hair splattered everywhere and the stunned creature crashed to the ground.

Seymour stood beside a massive spruce and thumped his chest in triumph. He gave a loud yell and a dozen other Green and Brown Sasquatch appeared from their hiding places. All held rocks at the ready.

The chief of the Greens had not forgotten the humans, especially the smallest one who had shared his mind. When the false Sasquatch had refused to follow him into the woods, Seymour had doubled back and watched them lead away their captives. After making sure Bertha and the other injured would be all right, he set out with several Sasquatch to rescue the humans.

The Bigfoot posse had no trouble staying unseen while they tracked their prey. This land had been their home for generations. They knew every tree and bush, every rock and ravine. Seymour realized too late that the chase would lead to the one cave in the entire region the Bigfoot never entered. If the false Sasquatch took their captives into that strange and sinister place, all was lost.

Seymour wanted to wait until dark before attacking since Bigfoot hunted and fought best at night. But with the sacred cave only a few yards away he had to do something. So he cast the first stone.

The Baron punched the air with his fist and shouted, "Yes!" over the fallen wraith. But his joy quickly vanished when the wounded Bigfoot shook his head and lurched to his feet. The oozing gash closed as if by reverse motion photography. All that remained of what should have been a fatal injury was a streak of blood in the beast's fur.

"He's still alive!" Jewel gasped.

This resurrection didn't shock Matterhorn. Dark spirits had supernatural strength; so why not miraculous healing power? He knew of only one thing that could kill a wraith—and he had sworn not to use it.

Emergency Exit

I F they had not been so close to the portal, the wraiths would have fought the Sasquatch and enjoyed killing them one at a time. But delivering the Talis took priority over personal pleasure. The wraith closest to Jewel roughly grabbed her with one hand and Nate with the other. He crouched behind the human shields and began backing uphill toward the portal. The wraith with the disappearing wound seized Matterhorn and the Baron and did the same.

Seymour was stunned by the recovery of the false Sasquatch. These evil creatures could not be stopped.

But not all the Bigfoot were paralyzed with awe. Thrower was perched on an outcrop above the cave as still as a gargoyle. When the wraith dragging the Baron got close, Thrower jumped. He landed like a rockslide on the wraith's back, knocking him down and jarring the humans loose.

The startled wraith spun and grabbed Thrower and the two became a blur of flying fur.

"Stop!" yelled the other wraith. He lifted Jewel by her braid like a puppeteer as he strode toward the fight.

Jewel reacted quickly to save her scalp by twisting herself around the Bigfoot's arm like a snake around a branch. Why did bullies always go for the hair, she wondered. She bit down hard on his thumb and kicked at his eyes.

The wraith stumbled and almost fell, more annoyed than hurt. He shook Jewel off and lifted a huge foot to crush her only to find the point of Matterhorn's Sword ready to make him a new navel.

"Come on and die!" Matterhorn threatened.

The beast backed off just as Thrower screamed.

Out of the corner of his eye, Matterhorn saw the Sasquatch fly through the air and splat headfirst into the rocks from which he had jumped. His eyes rolled back and he crumpled to the ground.

The Baron rushed to Thrower's side as the wraith scooped up a large stone and moved in to finish the job.

"Enough!" shouted the lead wraith. "Get the humans into the portal!" he commanded. "Now!"

His companion growled and hurled his rock an inch above Thrower's head. Stone chips sprayed everywhere, cutting the Baron's face.

The wraiths herded their hostages into the cave's open maw. Outside the Sasquatch watched in frustration. Seymour howled with rage at being unable to help those who had helped him. He scrambled upward to see if Thrower was dead or alive.

The wraiths answered with a howl of their own, a howl of triumph! Another few seconds and they would be out of this dreadful place.

The Sword in Matterhorn's hands grew brighter in the enveloping darkness.

"Put that out!" one of the wraiths cried.

"I'm not doing it," Matterhorn argued, taking advantage of the light to scope out the cave. The floor was smooth, the walls were scalloped with rough stones, and the ceiling was double-arched with a ridge down the middle. The wide passage doglegged left and Matterhorn was shoved into it. A few yards around the bend, he stopped.

"I can't go any farther," he said.

"Quit stalling!" the wraith screamed from behind.

"I'm not stalling. Someone's in my way."

"That's impossible!" the wraith fumed.

"I'm afraid not," said the man planted tree-like in the passage. He was tall, well built, and completely bald. His amber eyes had a deadly gleam.

"Who are you?" the wraith demanded. Without waiting for an answer, he pushed Matterhorn aside and charged the stranger, who dodged with the footwork of a boxer.

"You will have to do better than that," he chided, snapping a straight-fingered jab at his attacker's throat.

The Sasquatch jerked back with a partially crushed larynx.

The other wraith circled to the right of the unexpected intruder and motioned his injured companion to the left. He hated this animal body and was fed up with all these problems. This last delay on a mission that had already taken too long was the most disturbing. Where had this stranger come from? Did he know about the Talis?

The Bigfoot were now on opposite sides of the unmoving figure. At a nod they pounced in perfect unison, one lunging for the head while the other rolled into the feet.

The man didn't crumple under the onslaught; he vanished!

Jewel sensed there was someone behind them, and she spun to see the man standing by a niche in the wall. "This way!" he cried.

The other Travelers heard it, too, and raced toward the man. "In here," he said, waving then into the niche.

Jewel and Matterhorn skidded to a halt in confusion. The shallow recess was only a foot deep. The Baron kept going—right through solid rock.

The wraiths untangled themselves and rushed after the fleeing humans.

"Move it!" Nate yelled as he shoved Jewel and Matterhorn into the wall.

Epilogue

MATTERHORN didn't have time to protect his face from being smashed into the stone. But instead of hard rock, he felt a tightening slick surface as if he were being shrink-wrapped in plastic.

He could not move.

He could not breathe.

He was trapped between moments, suspended in time.

Is this what it feels like to be dead, he wondered? A light show danced across the outside of his clear envelope. There was no sense of motion inside. Then everything faded to deep black and he heard rustling. A wave of heat dried the sweat on his face. The darkness became a shade lighter.

"Where are we?" Jewel asked in a shaky voice.

Good, Matterhorn thought. He wasn't alone. And he probably wasn't dead. Before he could say anything, he heard the Baron reply, "I don't know. Wherever it is, let's hope the wraiths can't follow us. Matterhorn, are you okay?"

"I think so. Where's Nate?"

The question rang in the void like an unanswered phone.

As Matterhorn's eyes adjusted, he made out two shapes. There should have been three. Had Nate missed the magic exit? Had the wraiths grabbed him?

"What happened?" Jewel wanted to know. "Who was that stranger?"

"My name is Elok," came an unexpected response.

A shrouded shape glided in front of the Travelers. The man's smooth head and bull neck reminded Matterhorn of a brass bullet.

His movement raised a cloud of dust. Jewel coughed and said, "I have a feeling we're not in Kansas anymore."

Elok smiled. "Not even close."

Matterhorn was in no mood for guessing games. The harrowing events of the last week had made an omelet of his emotions. He had barely escaped drowning in a flooding volcano only to be captured by wraiths and forced to marched for a day. His broken arm hurt like crazy. His nerves were shot. He had just been shoved through a rock wall. "Where are we?" he demanded, raising his Sword. "Is this First Realm?"

"If it were," Elok replied, "you would be dead and that would be lost." He pointed at Matterhorn's Talis.

"How do you know that?" the Baron challenged as he stepped forward, switchwhip in hand.

"There is no cause for alarm," Elok said. His gaze moved from the Sword to the whip while his body remained relaxed. "I serve the Maker and the royals of the Realm. As to your present location, you are still on Earth. In Egypt to be precise."

Matterhorn let out a sigh and lowered the weapon. It remained lit and formed a halo around them.

"Thank you for saving us," Jewel said. She reached her right hand toward him in a Traveler's salute while concealing something in her left hand.

Elok leaned away and warned, "Do not be so quick to use the Band of Justice, especially on one who has given no cause for mistrust."

Jewel blushed at the exposure of her secret intent.

"Talis are not to be used lightly," Elok said. "Put the Band away and use your common sense. What does it tell you?"

Jewel did so and stared up into Elok's unblinking amber eyes. "You saved our lives," she sighed after a bit. "I suppose that's enough for now."

The Baron put away his switchwhip and shed his pack. "If you used a portal, then we're either in the Great Pyramid at Giza or in the Valley of the Kings. What time period?"

"We are in the Valley," Elok said. "1325 B.C., local time."

"What are we doing here?"

"Please sit," Elok motioned to a pile of dusty furniture. "I will explain."

"Not until I know what happened to Nate," Matterhorn said, splashing Sword-light this way and that. They were in a vaulted storeroom with what appeared to be life-size comics on the walls. Odd pieces of furniture and household items were piled everywhere, including clay pots full of decaying foodstuffs and reed hampers crammed with clothes.

"Calm down," Elok said. "Your companion has been watching from the shadows to see what I will do. Is that not so, Nate?"

"Maybe." Nate followed his voice into the light—and tripped on a carpet.

Elok caught the stumbling bushman. "Your caution is wise," he said.

Nate regained his feet and smiled. "Didn't have a chance to look before we leaped. Why Egypt?"

"My master and I are here on the business of the Realm," Elok said. "Business for which the Band of Justice would be of great help. Because we knew where it had been hidden I went to retrieve it."

"How did you know to show up when you did?" Matterhorn asked.

Elok ran a hand over his smooth scalp and admitted, "The timing was a divine coincidence. I did not foresee your arrival at the portal, or your need of rescue."

Matterhorn pondered this as he sat down against an elaborately carved trunk. The Talis were safe; that was the important thing for now.

But what was he doing in Egypt?

And how would he get home?

THE END